HARBINGERS

The Fog

Alton Gansky

**Bill Myers, Frank Peretti,
and Angela Hunt**

Published by Amaris Media International.

Copyright © 2015 Alton Gansky

Cover Design: Angela Hunt

Photo © Alton Gansky

ISBN: 0692544429

www.harbingersseries.com

HARBINGERS

A novella series by

Bill Myers, Frank Peretti, Angela Hunt, and Alton Gansky

In this fast-paced world with all its demands, the four of us wanted to try something new. Instead of the longer novel format, we wanted to write something equally as engaging but that could be read in one or two sittings—on the plane, waiting to pick up the kids from soccer, or as an evening's read.

We also wanted to play. As friends and seasoned novelists, we thought it would be fun to create a game we could participate in together. The rules were simple:

Rule 1

Each of us would write as if we were one of the characters in the series:

- Bill Myers would write as Brenda, the street-hustling tattoo artist who sees images of the future.
- Frank Peretti would write as the professor, the atheist ex-priest ruled by logic.
- Angela Hunt would write as Andi, the professor's brilliant-but-geeky assistant who sees inexplicable patterns.
- Alton Gansky would write as Tank, the naïve, big-hearted jock with a surprising connection to a healing power.

Rule 2

Instead of the four of us writing one novella together (we're friends but not crazy), we would write it like a TV series. There would be an overarching story line into which we'd plug our individual novellas, with each story written from our character's point of view.

Bill's first novella, *The Call*, sets the stage. It will be followed by Frank's, *The Haunted*, Angela's *The Sentinels*, and Alton's *The Girl*. And if we keep having fun, we'll begin a second round and so on until other demands pull us away or, as in TV, we get cancelled.

There you have it. We hope you'll find these as entertaining in the reading as we did in the writing.

Bill, Frank, Angie, and Al

THE FOG

By Alton Gansky

PROLOGUE

I KNOW THE people behind me are wondering what I'm doing. I can't blame them. It's not everyday you see a man my size standing on the parapet of a high-rise building in the middle of a major city and looking down at a street he can't see a mere fifty floors below. Did I mention it was night and the only light I have came from emergency lamps? Probably not. I'm not at my best at the moment.

I've never admitted this to anyone before, but I don't like heights that much. I don't let on, of course. A big football player isn't supposed to have such fears. Well, I ain't a football player anymore. I'm just a big ex-jock teetering on the edge some five hundred feet above the sidewalk below.

It's eerie up here. Not just because most of the lights in the city are out but because of the silence. About a million-and-a-half people call San Diego home, or so the professor tells me. He has a knack for such things.

When we first arrived, I noticed the noise of downtown: traffic, people talking, busses, mass transit trains, and other noise-making things of humanity. Now all I can hear is the sound of a gentle breeze pushing at my back and zipping by my ears. That and the sobs of my friends.

If all of that wasn't enough to raise the hair on a man's neck, there was the fog—a fog like I've never seen before. At first it looked like your garden variety mist, but it moved differently, and—how do I say this—it was populated. Things lived in it. Bad things. Horrible things. Ugly things.

When I look down I can't see the street, just the roof of the fog bank. That and the things swimming in it.

A face appeared.

I shuddered.

It wasn't alone.

The things swam in the fog like dolphin swim in the ocean. Except dolphins are cute. These are no dolphins. No siree. These things ain't from around here. They're not from anywhere on this earth. I can only guess where they call home, but if it was Hell, I'd believe it with no hesitation.

"Tank…"

Even with my back to her, I recognize Andi's voice. I would recognize it anywhere and at anytime. The biggest hurricane couldn't keep her words from my ears.

I raised a hand. I didn't want to hear it. I wanted to hear it more than anything I've ever wanted. I know it doesn't make sense, but I'm a guy standing on the edge of certain death, so my thinking, such as it is, has a few hiccups. Don't expect me to make a lot of sense at the moment. You stand on the edge of a high-rise an inch from death and see how well the gears in your head work.

I allowed myself one last glance back. I turned slowly to look at my friends and the scores of people standing behind them. I was real careful. When I go over the edge, I want it to be my decision, not a fool mistake.

My gaze first fell on Professor McKinney, worldwide lecturer, atheist, and former Catholic priest. Yep, he's a bit conflicted. He's the smartest man I've ever met, and at times, the biggest pain in my fanny. He is retirement age but hasn't slowed down. Good thing. The team needs him. He stared at me through his glasses. Even in the dim light provided by a pale ivory moon overhead and the emergency lighting, I saw something I had never seen before: a tear in his eye.

The professor's hand rested on Andi Goldstein's shoulder. I let my gaze linger on her. My gaze *always* lingered on her. Her usually wild red hair might strike some as a bit strange, but she was fashion-model beautiful to me. There were tears running down her face. The sight of them squeezed my heart like a man might squeeze a lemon.

Next to her stood Brenda Barnick. Her black face seldom showed a smile and she could put on an expression that would melt steel. I've faced a lot of big guys on the football field, but not one of them put any fear in me. When Brenda lost her temper she plain scared me and anyone else within the sound of her voice. She's a street smart tattoo artist, all hard on the outside, but I know she has a great big heart. She looked away but not before I saw the fear and pain on her face.

One way I know Brenda has a big heart is the boy standing in front of her. The kid has mental problems. Well, that's what the doctors say, but we know better.

He's just different. And talented. Brenda, through a lie or two, got herself named his guardian. She makes a good mom.

The sight of my friends gutted me. I turned from them. It was easier looking at what I feared rather than those I love. I was on this ledge for them and for many others.

I raised my right foot and inched it over the edge of the parapet. The breeze pushed at me as if encouraging me to jump.

The things in the fog were agitated, like sharks in bloody water. Their small, lethal heads bobbed up and down in the fog.

They were waiting.

Waiting for me to lean forward.

I did.

A hundred pairs of clawed hands reached for me.

But first, I need to tell you how I got here.

ALL DRESSED UP WITH
SOMEWHERE TO GO

OF ALL THE things I've seen lately, and I've seen a lot, today might just take the cake. I've seen a house that appears and disappears at will; I've seen the inside of the Vatican; I've seen flying orbs made of living metal (that's what Andi calls it); I've seen a green fungus that invades living things and takes them over; I've been chased by monsters not of this world and protected a little girl who grew younger with time instead of older. But this. Seriously. This is almost too much. I would think I was dreaming if I weren't standing and lookin' into a mirror in my hotel room.

Still, I can't deny it. The image was right there in the mirror: me—in a tuxedo. I'm a simple kinda guy. I like meat and potatoes, vanilla ice cream, and have been known to watch a little NASCAR racing from time to time. I figured I'd have to wear a tux if I ever got married, but maybe not even then. I skipped the proms at school so I never had a need to rent one of these monkey suits.

There was my image: all six-foot-three, 260 pounds of me—in a tux!

Someone pounded on my door. "Let's get a move on, Tank. The car and driver are waiting."

The professor. Dr. James McKinney is our leader although we never elected him. He makes many of the decisions because, at sixty he's the oldest; because he is smart, educated, and domineering. He's a priest who lost faith and left the church. Instead of conducting Mass, he spent his time traveling the country proving God doesn't exist, faith is a dream, and believers are fools. His word, not mine. Yep, despite all that stupidity the guy is the smartest man I know. Still, I like him.

"Do I have to kick the door in, Tank?"

I smiled. I'd kinda like to see him try. "Coming."

I turned from the mirror, glad to leave my image behind and opened the door. He had his arms crossed, wore a tux similar to mine, and flashed his well-known frown at me. He was tall, full head of gray hair, and eyes that seemed to look through people and things.

He studied me for a moment, relaxed, and lowered his arms to his side. The corners of his mouth ticked-up a coupla notches.

"For a star football player, you clean up nicely."

"I was a good college player, but never a star. You know that, Professor." That was as true as sunshine in the morning. I played well in high school, and my first two years of college weren't too shabby. When I transferred to the University of Washington on a football scholarship things changed. I had been playing for a junior college in Southern California and lovin' it, but playing for a major university with a well-known football team was an eye-opener. I was playing with and against people who made me look small. The hits were harder; the plays more complicated; the competition out of this world. I was a tiny fish in a great big pond.

Then I got hurt. A 300-pound lineman did a dance step on my foot and I was out for the season. To make things worse, our little team of do-gooders was traveling more, facing greater unknowns, and risking our lives. Somehow, football just didn't seem important anymore. I haven't touched a football since last December. People told me I'd miss it. Maybe I do a little, but I need to be here, with this team doing what, apparently, only we can.

"Do I have this on right?" I asked the professor.

"Your bowtie is loose. Turn around."

I did an about turn and felt the professor fiddlin' with the adjustable bow tie. It tightened.

"Can you still breathe?"

"Yes."

"Okay, so not tight enough then."

"Hey."

"Just kidding, Tank." He had me turn around again. "Perfect. You look like James Bond."

"I look like a penguin on steroids."

"Nonsense, son. Besides, people like penguins."

"Are you gonna be ridin' my case all night, Professor."

"Most of the night, anyway. Come on. You're in for a surprise."

13

I hoped it was a good one. We've had our fill of bad surprises.

The Marriott Courtyard was a cut above most hotels, but not fancy. The professor called it a business hotel, but I saw plenty of people who didn't look like executives. I didn't bother to point that out. I was just glad for a nice place to stay. In the early days, we often had to rely on the professor to pay for airline tickets, food, and the like. These days, someone was taking care of such things. Don't ask who. I don't know. None of us do. Not yet.

We rode the elevator down three floors to the lobby. Seated on a sofa situated across from the desk was a young woman with vivid red hair. Andi normally let her hair hang whatever way it chose, but not tonight. She had spent part of the day at the beauty parlor, but to me there was nothing they could do to improve on perfection. I may have been wrong. Her hair had been pulled, woven, whatever they did in such shops, close to her head. She wore an evening dress of white and black stripes that were set on the diagonal. The dress left one shoulder bare. Not being an expert in such matters, I have no idea how a designer would describe it. I settled for, "Wow."

Andrea Goldstein (we just call her Andi) rose from the sofa and all the air left the room. She seldom wore make up, but tonight she proved she had skills that went beyond computers and patterns.

She straightened the dress. "Do I look all right?"

She was looking at me. I cleared my throat and wondered if I should comment on the dress, her hair, her make up, her beauty, so I said, "Um, wow!"

The professor chuckled, something he seldom does. "It's okay, Andi, I speak fluent Tank. He says you look gorgeous."

"Yeah, what he said." I've never been quick.

Andi smiled in away that nearly melted my spine. "Mr. Bjorn Christensen cleans up pretty good too."

"Here that, Tank? She thinks you look like James Bond, too."

"I didn't say that, Professor." Andi's smile widened. "But you do, Tank."

I hoped for all I was worth that I wouldn't blush.

I blushed.

The professor's expression soured. "Where's Barnick? Do I have to go get her too?"

"Of course not, old man."

The voice came from behind us. A very familiar voice. I turned and got another shock. Brenda Barnick looked like she had just stepped from a model's catwalk. Her dress was white on top and contrasted with her ebony skin. Gold lace something or another separated the floor length black dress. She too had spent time getting her hair done. She wore dreadlocks most of the time. Of course, she still had those, but somehow the hairdresser worked some kinda magic. For a streetwise tattoo artist, she looked like a movie star.

"Give us a spin," Andi said.

Brenda did. It was a tad wobbly. "I hate these shoes. They make no sense."

"No worries, girl. You'll get the hang of heels. All you have to do is shut out the rest of the world and focus on your feet."

"That should make the evening fun for me," Brenda said.

A movement behind Brenda caught my attention. "That you, Daniel?"

No response.

"Come on, dude," I pressed. "I'm wearing one too."

Daniel was the youngest member of our team. Just ten-years-old and a year ago he was spending much of his time in a mental institution for children. Apparently telling people you have invisible friends only you can see is not a good idea. He has no parents. He was alone, until he appeared on our doorstep. Daniel, has been a lifesaver several times. Brenda has, so she tells, been declared his guardian. She introduces him to others as her son. They usually look at his white face, then at her black skin. When that happens, she narrows her eyes and says, "What?" Brenda is tough. I think she could cower a rhino just by staring at it.

Despite her tough exterior, Brenda had a heart of gold. She was a natural mother and she took care of Daniel as if she had given birth to him.

I stepped to Daniel and held out my fist. He smiled and started our secret handshake. Fortunately, he chose the short one. The long one takes two full minutes.

"Now that we're done looking at ourselves, it's time to go." The professor pointed at the entry doors. A long, black limo pulled up.

First a tuxedo. Now a limo. It all should be fun. I doubted it would be.

It never was.

Chapter 2

SQUARE PEGS

THE LIMO WAS long and black and shiny. I'm a pickup guy, Chevy if you must know, but once inside the Ford I began to change my mind. Like I said, I'm a simple guy but a man could get used to this. The car was a Ford Excursion that looked as if someone had spent a year or two stretching the thing so—I counted the seats—fourteen people could fit inside. It looked expensive. It smelled expensive.

Our seat was a long, deeply padded bench that wrapped around the back of the vehicle and ran along one side of the passenger area. A simulated wood bar ran along the other side. Once in and comfy, the professor and Brenda wasted no time in helping themselves to the wine. There was even a soda for Daniel. Me, I passed. I've never been good with liquor. Something Brenda knows since I let myself get talked into drinking something I shouldn't. When I came to, I learned my football friends had dumped me off in a tattoo parlor. That's were I first met Brenda and got my first and only tattoo. I wasn't conscious during the tattooing. I've stayed away from booze ever since.

I glanced at Daniel. He was in awe. He held his soda but showed little interest in it. There was too much to see. A small brochure awaited us and I glanced through it. "Hey Daniel, this car's got four televisions. Four, little dude."

His eyes widened. Daniel doesn't talk much. He's certainly capable of it, he just chooses not to. Much of the time he seems lost in a world only he can see, or playing a video game on his smartphone. I've even heard him talk to people who aren't there. No, that's not quite right. He talks to people the rest of us can't see. Don't get me wrong. The little guy is not nuts. His invisible friends have helped us a few times in the past.

The limo pulled from the hotel and onto the street. Our hotel was in a San Diego suburb called Kearny Mesa. Our destination was downtown proper. The professor told us to expect a twenty-minute drive, maybe longer. It was Friday night and he had been told traffic could back up anywhere along the path. Since we were headed to a party, we didn't have to be there on the stroke of seven.

Night had settled like a thick blanket so the professor turned on the overhead lights.

"Okay," he said. He spoke just above a whisper. "We have a few minutes for review. Andi?"

Andi Goldstein, still so pretty she hurt my eyes, and my heart, shifted in her seat and pulled a set of folded papers from her purse—the kind of purse women call a clutch.

"We've gone over this before so I'm going to be quick. We're going to Krone & Associates. It's an architecture firm. That you know. I've spent part of the day gathering information. I had to do it at the hair salon but I found what I needed. Gotta love smartphones."

She passed one page to each of us. On the page were some photos and a brief history of Krone & Associates.

"Krone is our primary concern," the professor said. "At least that's what I glean from the little information our handlers give us." He pressed his lips into a line. "One of these days, we're gonna find out who they are."

"Focus, Dr. McKinney." Andi was one of the few people who talk to the professor that way. She had been his assistant for several years and traveled with him while he tried to convince the world there is no God, that religion is for fools, and that smart people know that. I don't know it. I'm a Christian myself and I don't hide that. Naturally, I irritate the professor a good deal. There's some satisfaction in that.

"You tell, 'em, girl," Brenda said. She was the other one who spoke her mind to the professor. Andi earned the right; Brenda just didn't care what the professor thought.

"Krone & Associates has been in existence for thirty years and is responsible for scores of large building projects. About twenty years ago, the firm broke into the high-rise design business by winning a contest for a skyscraper to be built in Houston. They won a couple of contracts after that and pretty soon businesses wanting a high-rise with their name on it came calling. Now bear in mind, much of this comes from their website, so it may be filled with PR fluff."

"No doubt," the professor said.

Brenda found a small bowl of cheese and another of tiny crackers. "Snacks!"

That woman can eat and never gain weight.

Andi pressed on, snacks not withstanding. The president of the company is Allen Krone, as you might guess. His wife is Janice. Those are the first two photos. Both are sixty years old."

"Ancient," Daniel said. Then he smiled. I only mention that because he does it so seldom.

"Watch it, young man." The professor straightened. "I happen to be sixty-years-old."

"Ancient," Daniel repeated.

Even the professor had to grin.

Andi cleared her throat. "If I may have everyone's attention including young Daniel and Old Man McKinney."

"Ooh, nice one, girl," Brenda said. "That moniker could stick."

"It better not." McKinney didn't bother to look up from the page. It was if he was vacuuming the information into his brain. The man never seemed to forget anything or anyone. Kinda scary.

"Like many architecture firms, at least from what I can tell from the websites I visited, Krone & Associates has other partners."

"Let me guess," Brenda said. "Krone & Associates has, well, associates."

"Nothing gets by you, Barnick," the prof said.

"Straight up, Doc."

Andi sighed then plowed ahead. "The firm has two associates. I think they're called 'principals' in the trade. The next photo on your page is Jonathan Waterridge. He's forty and been with the firm for the last decade. I couldn't find out what firm or firms he served once he left the University of Southern California School of Architecture. In fact, he's barely a blip on the Internet. It's like he's allergic to the Web."

"The woman is his wife?" the professor asked.

"Yes. Her name is Helen. I imagine she'll be at the party tonight. I couldn't find out much about her either."

The limo slowed on the freeway. The professor's source about San Diego traffic was right. We were surrounded by sedans, sports cars, a Humvee, and an eighteen-wheeler. Drivers and passengers stared at us. Now I know why limos have tinted windows.

"The third partner is Ebony Watt, age forty-five."

"A woman architect?" I said. A chill filled the limo. The professor stared. Andi and Brenda glared at me. "Don't get me wrong. I think that's great." The temperature dropped another five degrees. I sighed.

"She's black too, Cowboy," Brenda said. "You wanna comment on that while you're at it?"

At least she called me Cowboy. That was her favorite term for me. I've heard her use stronger, less complimentary terms for people.

"I didn't mean that as it sounded. I just meant... How do I get out of this?"

"Tank, this is one of those times when silence is golden."

"Understood, Professor. I'm shutting up now."

"Ebony Watt came to the company from an architecture firm in Los Angeles. She graduated from UCLA with a degree in Architecture and Urban Design. She also has a degree in interior design. I found out more about her than I did for Waterridge. She's been featured in *Architectural Record* and other industry magazines. Oh, and I found this interesting, her husband is Eddy Bruce Watt."

The last statement floated on a sea of silence. I started to ask who Eddy Bruce Watt is, but kept my promise of silence.

"Really?" Andi said. "Seriously? None of you know Eddy Bruce Watt? The blues player. You've heard of B.B. King, right?"

We all admitted to knowing King.

"Okay, Eddy has been described as a younger B.B. King."

"If you say so," Brenda said. "I've never been a big blues fan."

The traffic began to move faster and Andi took that as an excuse to move on. "The retirement party is a pretty big deal among some San Diego executives and politicos. Who knows, maybe the mayor will show up."

"What's *her* name?" I said. Another silence. "You see what I did there? Did ya?" I plaster on my biggest smile.

"Nice, Cowboy," Brenda said. "There may be hope for you yet."

"It feels good knowing that my friends would consent to be seen in public with me."

"Hang on, Cowboy. I didn't say that."

"To answer your question, Tank," Andi said, "I didn't look up the mayor's name. I'll do that if he or she shows up."

Andi began collecting the papers she had passed out a short time ago. "It wouldn't be good to take these in with us. It might look like we're a team of stalkers. Okay, last thing from me. This is more than a retirement party. Allen Krone is passing the torch to his partners. He will formally announce the new name of the firm: Krone, Waterridge, and Watt. As founder, his name stays on the letterhead, but the real business will be handled by others."

DOWNTOWN SAN DIEGO oozed with cars and pedestrians. Some of the streets were one way. Taxis slithered through lines of traffic. Pedestrians crossed at intersections, some even waiting their turn, others, not so much. It seemed every corner had a nightclub, bar, restaurant, fast-food joint or some combination of those. Friday night was a busy time in the big city.

I watched the people on the street. There were men and women wearing nice clothes—not a tux mind you. They seemed too bright for that. Others wore their best bar-hopping rags. Many women wore skirts. Some were tiny. Others were tight. Some were both. Mixed in the group were a number of people with dirty, tattered clothing, uncombed and filthy hair, and carrying bags of what I assumed were all their worldly possessions. They moved through the streets paying no attention to the partiers; the partiers returned the favor. It was if two worlds shared the same space and the people of one could not talk to the people of the other. There was a sadness in seeing that. Doesn't seem right to stare at the homeless from inside a limo.

The driver showed great skill driving through the obstacle course of cars and pedestrians. He turned each corner as if he were steering a Volkswagen instead of a limo the size of an oceangoing barge. I hoped the professor would give the guy a big tip.

A Plexiglas window separated the driver's area from the passenger compartment. I was beginning to wonder how we would know when we were getting near when a voice came over speakers hidden in the limo's ceiling.

"We're pulling up to the building now," the driver said. "Someone will get the door for you."

I was stunned. It was a woman's voice. I had assumed the driver was male. You can bet I kept that little assumption to myself. Of course the driver had opened the door for us at the hotel, but I paid him, I mean her, no mind. I was blinded by the limo. Pretty dumb, I know.

"Thank you, driver," the professor said. I had to admit, he was smooth. He acted like he was used to being carted around in a limo.

The vehicle slowed to a stop, but was still several feet from the curb. I guess one didn't parallel park a car like this. As soon as the wheels stopped rolling the door opened.

A man in a doorman's uniform said, "Welcome to the Portal Bay Front Plaza. I hope you had a pleasant drive." He held the door while he stood to the side. That was the first thing I noticed. The second thing was the man's blue skin.

Yeah, that set me back a little, then I noticed the street and the sidewalk were also blue. When we exited the limo I learned why: our destination was a high-rise with a glass skin. All the glass was cobalt blue.

"Wow," Brenda said. She tilted her head back. "I'm impressed. How tall is this thing?" Brenda had no problem striking up conversations with strangers.

The doorman closed the door and the limo slowly pulled away. "Technically, ma'am, it is a fifty-story structure."

"Technically?" Andi always wants details.

"Yes, ma'am. It is forty-eight-stories above grade and two-stories below. FAA regulations."

As he said "FAA" a commercial airliner flew overhead. The doorman smiled as if he had planned that. "San Diego International Airport isn't far from here. The Federal Aviation Administration limits all buildings in the flight path to 500 feet or less."

"And fifty-stories sounds better than forty-eight. Is that it?" Brenda said.

"I couldn't say ma'am." He nodded and offered a Hollywood smile. "This way please."

He led. We followed. "You look good in blue, Tank," Andi said. "Hey Brenda, can you use your magic tattoo ink to turn Tank blue?"

"I'd be willing to experiment."

Apparently I wasn't out of the doghouse yet.

I glanced at the building. I was too close to it to see all the detail but what I could see was amazing. The front to the building was glowing blue glass as I said, but part way up was a different floor. A single story was dark green. It split the building with maybe one-third of the floors below the glowing green band, and two-thirds above. At least the best I could tell.

The doorman opened the front door to the lobby. I say front door, but it was more than one door. There were several doors set in a wall of glass. Pretty sleek. I said he opened the door to the lobby, but he didn't really. He opened the door to a massive foyer. The building was tall with straight lines like giant refrigerator box set on end, but there was more to it than that. The big part of the building was set back from the street with the entrance—an extension that was as curvy as the rest of the building was straight—protruded to nearly the edge of the sidewalk.

We walked into the wide, glass foyer. I caught sight of the professor slipping some folding money to the doorman who took it without hesitation.

The ceiling of the foyer was curved as were its walls. It was like walking into a bubble. Pretty neat. As soon as the door closed behind us, the outside sounds disappeared, replaced by a soothing bubbling of a fountain directly ahead. A single, spiraling shaft rose from the wide fountain eight feet in the air or so and spurted out a gentle flow of water that fell into the fountain's pool. The water was blue—I should say, it appeared blue. More lighting tricks. The spiral spout was jade green.

A set of wide steps waited in front of us. There were only three risers.

"Interesting," Andi said.

Of course, I had to ask. "What?"

"Look at the tiles on the floor. Maybe they're called pavers, whatever. There are fifty tiles across the lobby. They're all blue marble—probably fake marble—except for the green ones that form a line." She studied the floor for a few moments. We didn't bother her. This is what Andi does. She sees patterns in almost everything. Seeing patterns in the floor tile would surprise no one who knew her.

"Each tile is about a foot square. That means the foyer is fifty-feet wide. Fifty. Like the number of stories in the building. And the green tiles start in the thirteenth row and run up the steps—"

"Like the green band on the outside of the building," I said.

"Listen to you, Cowboy, going all Andi on us." Brenda seemed impressed.

I shrugged. "It's hard to miss."

"I saw that too." Andi nodded. "I think the band would the thirteenth floor. They carried the theme into the building."

"It's just consistency in design." The professor could be dismissive. "It's part of the theme."

"If you say so." Andi seemed a little miffed. "I'm just bringing it up."

We walked up the three rows of steps, past the fountain and into a much wider and taller space. The real lobby. People wandered about, many of the men in the same kind of tuxedo straight jacket I was wearing.

"This place is amazing," I said. I was looking at the ceiling. Somehow, long glowing strips of light ran the width of the ceiling. This light was white and was the only illumination I saw. Curved blue couches were tucked here and there. The backs of the sofas were low and streamlined. The dark blue tile transitioned into rows of ever lighter blue until all the blue was gone and a few rows of white were left. Those ran in front of a wide desk like those in a fancy hotel. Several men and women stood behind the counter-high desk talking to guests. Behind the counter area were two tall structures that looked suspiciously like the building we were in. They even had the green stripe.

"You know, I once thought about being an architect." The professor seemed to be sucking the sights in through his eyes. I studied it for a bit, but then got derailed by seminary." He shook his head. "I should have stayed the course. I would have been of more use to society as an architect than I was as a priest."

When we first became a team—at the time we didn't know we were a team—I would have argued with him. Never did any good. Besides, this wasn't the place to start a conversation that put him in a bad mood. He had been almost fun to be around this evening. Not something I could say most times.

"But if you did that, Professor, then you would have missed out on meeting me."

The professor glanced at Brenda. "I think you have that backwards, Barnick. You would have had to miss me." He paused. "Either way, we both might have been better off."

And there it was. Dr. James McKinney had—just like old milk—turned sour. Brenda didn't respond and for that I will forever be thankful.

Something else caught my eye. Spaced around the large lobby were glowing, blue trees. Not real trees, because, trees don't usually glow. These were like sculptures—art. Each tree stood about five feet tall, had no leaves, and looked as if they were made of glass. As cool as the whole lobby was, those tree-things were the coolest. If I were a thief, I'd have spent a little time trying to figure out how to sneak one of those babies out the front door. It would make a great nightlight for Daniel.

Daniel was looking at them too. "Pretty great, right little dude?"

He didn't answer. Nothing new there. He did however look puzzled. Not afraid. Just confused. He's a smart kid so I knew I didn't need to tell them they weren't real trees. Maybe he was trying to figure out how they worked. I would have told him. If I knew how they worked.

We followed the professor to the long curved desk behind which stood three people in dark suits: two women, and one man.

"Dr. James McKinney and party." The professor had chosen one of the women to speak to. She had very blue eyes. So blue I suspected they were contact lenses. He reached into an inside pocket of his tuxedo coat and removed five invitations. They looked like tickets to a movie or something.

She smiled, took the invitations and scanned them with one of those laser scanners you see in some stores. This scanner looked a little more high-tech. "Thank you, Dr. McKinney." She handed one invitation back to him.

"Ms. Barnick?" the receptionist said.

"Yo."

The professor cringed.

The blue-eyed woman handed an invitation to Brenda. "Please keep these with you at all times. They are part of the security system." She handed back the rest of the invitations. She hesitated when she saw Daniel but only for a moment. I guess she wasn't expecting four adults to walk in with a kid.

Speaking of security. At each end of the check-in counter stood a man in a gray suit coat. Both were about my size and each wore a security badge. The one on the right nodded at me. It was what one jock did when meeting another.

We were directed to the elevators at the back of the lobby and told to use the one on the right. It was one of six elevators.

As we approached the elevator I asked why we had to take the one on the right.

"Most likely," the professor said, "the others don't open on the top floor."

Made sense to me.

Before we could press the up button on the panel next to the elevator, the doors opened for us.

Andi stopped in her tracks. "It's like it sensed our presence."

"I think it did." The professor continued into the elevator cab. "I bet our invitations have RFID chips."

Brenda and I gave the professor a puzzled look.

"You wanna explain that, McKinney?"

I'm glad Brenda asked. Sometimes I get tired of being the one who doesn't know anything, although I know more than most people think.

"RFID. Radio Frequency Identification. It's used for many things including security badges. The elevator knows we are near and that we have the right invitations."

"Of course," Brenda said. "So they can track us."

"That's a little paranoid, Barnick." The professor paused as we stepped into the elevator cab. "But yes, they can."

TOP FLOOR PARTY

THE ELEVATOR WAS completely red inside. Like the building, like the fake trees in the lobby, the walls glowed. Since coming here I had been blue and now red.

"Odd," Andi said.

"Uh oh, here it comes." Brenda and Andi got along pretty good, but no one was protected from Brenda's quips. "Whatcha got, Pattern Girl."

"Again with the Pattern Girl, Brenda? Really?"

"Sorry."

She didn't sound sorry to me. "What is it, Andi?"

She pointed at the control panel. "There's no floor thirteen. Either someone can't count or they're a tad on the superstitious side."

The professor grunted. "Most likely the latter. It used to be customary to avoid the number thirteen in buildings. It's called triskaidekaphobia."

No one question the professor about the term but that didn't stop him. "The word means fear of thirteen."

30

"Good to know," Brenda said. "I could be on *Jeopardy* someday."

The professor grunted his doubt. Sadly, he goes through more ups and downs than this elevator.

I looked at the panel. Andi was right: eleven, twelve, fourteen. "So there's no thirteenth floor?"

The professor sighed. "Think about it, Tank. Of course there's a thirteenth floor. It's just not numbered thirteen, that or the floor is occupied by one of the companies that share ownership of the building and they have their own elevator."

"Why would they do that?" I had a good idea, but nothing puts the professor in a better mood than when he feels like he's enlightening us.

"To keep people from accidently going to the floor. Perhaps it's a government agency that doesn't want foot traffic—"

"Like spies and stuff?" Daniel asked.

The doctors could say what they want about Daniel's mental and emotional problems but he didn't miss a trick.

"Could be, son. Could be. Or maybe something a little more boring. Anyway, there are many reasons this elevator might not have a button for the thirteenth floor. For all we know, that floor could be used for all the equipment that keeps a building like this working. You wouldn't want people accidentally popping into a place like that. Especially in the age of terrorism."

"I still think it's weird." Brenda tugged at her evening gown. She looked great but I was pretty sure this was the first time she had worn fancy duds like this. I didn't feel so alone.

"Zebras." The professor's one-word comment caught us all off guard.

"Zebras?" Brenda said. "You have a thing for zebras?"

Again the professor sighed. He was a master at it. He had taken the art of sighing to new heights. It had become a game with us: can we get him to sigh in some new way.

"First thing doctors learn in med school is this: When you hear the sound of hoof beats, think horses not zebras."

I decided to take a stab at interpretation. "So, look for the common and not the unusual?"

"Spot on, Tank."

My first impulse was to remind everyone that we had seen quite a few zebras since we were thrown together.

The elevator slowed and the doors parted to reveal a wide and open room. No walls. A person could see from one end of the building to the other. Windows surrounded us on three sides. Only the rear wall was solid. Blue light spilled in through the glass but was much dimmer than what I had seen outside. Scores of people milled around the open space. The men wore tuxedos and the women evening dresses. We fit right in. Even little Daniel.

There dozens of the glow-light trees we had seen in the lobby. In the center of the room was a wide and very long table that supported a couple dozen model buildings, including a mock up of the one we were in. Some were much taller, apparently built out of the way of commercial airlines. I first noticed the model of the building we were in, then I noticed an odd, narrow, pyramid like building. It didn't seem to fit with the others. It was dark, colored with black and browns. Kinda gave me the creeps.

Nearby stood several short partitions, all red like the insides of the elevator. Attached to those were a bunch of large photos. Even at a distance, I could see they were portraits of Allen Krone, the head of the architecture company.

"Welcome." The word came from a woman approaching from our left. Unlike the other women in the room, she wore... I guess you'd call it a waiter's uniform. "My name is Mable. I'm one of the greeters."

She didn't look like a Mable. She had straight black hair, bangs that hung to her perfect eyebrows, and the same kind of blue eyes the receptionist had.

"Good evening, Mable. I'm Dr. McKinney and these are my good friends Andi Goldstein, Brenda Barnick, Bjorn Christensen, and this little man is Daniel."

Daniel scooted closer to Brenda.

The runway model/greeter smiled. "I'm very glad to meet you and I know Mr. Krone is pleased you responded to his invitation."

None of us mentioned the fact that we hadn't been invited by Mr. Krone.

Mable bent forward without bothering to bend her knees. Her face was pointed at Daniel, the rest of her was pointed—elsewhere. Andi and Brenda exchanged glances. I did the same with the professor. We chose not to speak.

"You look so handsome in that tuxedo, Daniel," Mable said. "I know there are a lot of adults around here but that's okay. I made sure there was ice cream and cake for special guests like you. Just let me know when you're ready and I'll make sure you get a big bowl." She straightened. "If that's all right?" She looked at each of us.

Brenda answered. "It's fine with me as long as I get some too."

Mable's smile widened. "There's plenty. This is a party after all." She motioned around the room. "Please feel free to explore. We have an exhibit of some of the more interesting buildings the firm has done and a portrait gallery of Mr. Krone through the years. There is a snack table on the east side with chocolate covered strawberries, caviar, and many other treats. Next to it is a hosted bar. The wines are especially good.

"Exits are clearly marked as are the restrooms. If you have any questions, you'll find other greeters and hostesses wandering the floor. We've all dressed alike so we will be easy to find."

A mild tone sounded behind us and the elevator doors opened. In the short time we had been chatting, or rather Mable had been chatting, the elevator had retrieved more guests.

I looked at the professor. He looked at Andi. Andi looked at Brenda. Brenda looked at me.

"I'm startin' to feel a tad conspicuous just standing here," I said. "What do we do now?" I looked at the professor again. He shrugged. Some leader.

"Kinda makes you wish you knew why were here, doesn't it?" Brenda said.

"We never know until we're in the thick of it." Andi spoke just above a whisper.

"That's the fun of it." Brenda pulled at her dress again. "I think this thing is trying to squeeze the life out of me."

"Think of it as a long lasting hug." Andi said that with a grin.

"That's a creepy thought."

Brenda isn't the huggin' type. Except with Daniel. He's gotten his fair share of hugs from her. But then again, he's Daniel.

"Speaking of Daniel," I said.

Andi hiked an eyebrow. "We weren't talking about Daniel."

"I know; I was thinking . . ." I said. "Never mind. Where is he?"

Brenda glanced to her side. He wasn't there. "He was just here." I heard the concern in her voice.

"He's okay. I mean, where could he have gone? Let's spread out. Andi you check the food area, maybe he went for the promised ice cream. Tank, you check the bathroom—"

"Excuse me."

The voice deep but a little weak. I turned. There was Daniel standing three feet away holding the hand of a dapper gray haired old gent.

"It seems this young man wants us to meet."

His words flowed easily and I could hear some humor in them.

"Daniel!" Brenda cleared her throat. "What are you doing?" She made eye contact with the man. Daniel continued to hold onto the gentleman's hand. "I hope he wasn't a bother, sir."

Another smile. "Not at all. He has been every bit the gentleman."

Daniel smiled. Then the light in my brain went on. Daniel had just found the star of the party: Allen Krone. Well, I least one of us could make a decision.

Brenda was a leaf in a hurricane. "He-He just walked up and began talking to you?"

"Yes. Very friendly child." Krone extended his hand to Brenda. "I'm Allen Krone. Welcome to my retirement party."

Brenda shook his hand. "I'm embarrassed, I mean. Brenda. Brenda Barnick. I'm Daniel's guardian." It took another second for Brenda to take her foot off the throttle of her brain. She made introductions, introducing the professor last. At least she did right by him, calling him "Dr. James McKinney."

"Doctor McKinney. MD?" Daniel finally let go of Krone's hand.

"No. PhD. Academic doctorate." The professor shifted gears. "This is a lovely building. You must be very proud of it."

Krone's smile widened. "I am. Of course, I owe my partners a great deal of the credit. I confess to overseeing the aesthetics, but Jonathan and Ebony handled the interiors and structural details." Then, as if an afterthought, said, "Jonathan Waterridge and Ebony Watt, the other principals in the firm."

Andi had already told us their names so they weren't new to us.

He pointed to a small group near the center of the room. "That's them over there. With the mayor and his wife."

Jonathan Waterridge was tall, maybe six-two or so, thin, and had a fairly large nose. Not huge, but large enough to guarantee he took a ribbin' when he was a kid. The mayor was not tall but he was stout. What he lacked in height he made up for in girth. His wife looked half his age, a third his width, and flashed platinum blond curls.

A motion to my right caught my attention. Daniel had moved to Brenda's side and was pulling on her dress. She took his hand in self-defense. If my little buddy pulled any more we all might see more of Brenda than we had ever seen before.

"Excuse me. Daniel was promised some ice cream and it seems he wants it right now."

"Certainly." Krone dipped his head as if bowing.

Brenda and Daniel moved to the refreshment area.

"You know," Krone began, "I'm having trouble remembering where we last met—"

The professor didn't let the man finish. No doubt he wanted to avoid the question Krone was going to ask. "I was just telling my friends that I had considered architecture as a career. I went another direction but I still have a great interest in the art and the science you practice. I wonder if you would indulge me and tell me a little about the wonderful building models."

"Of course." Krone looked around the room as if looking for someone to save him from a task he had probably done a dozen times this evening. He was stuck with the professor. The two moved away.

"That was slick," I said to Andi.

"The professor is nothing if not slick."

"What now?"

Andi shrugged. "That ice cream idea sounded good."

I agreed.

FOGGY NIGHT

"HOW'S THE ICE cream, buddy?" I looked at two chocolate scoops in his bowl. It was a real bowl too, not one of those plastic things you see at most parties. Someone would be doin' a lot of dishes when this shindig was over.

"Good."

"Is that bowl for me?" I pretended to reach toward his little treasure.

"Nope. Get your own."

"That's my boy." Brenda held her own bowl of frozen chocolate goodness. "You tell 'em."

I grinned and patted Daniel on the head. "I like a man who stands up for himself."

"He gets it from me," Brenda said.

"No doubt." Andi moved to the counter, learned there was red velvet cake for the having and asked for

38

some. "I'm really starting to love this get together." She took a bite of food and closed her eyes. I assumed it meant she was in cake heaven.

When she opened her eyes she asked Brenda, "How much of this stuff can we eat before our gowns come apart at the seams."

"Only one way to find out."

I have known these two women long enough to know that neither would overeat. They talked a good game, but always quit early. Me on the other hand...

"Sick."

It was Daniel. Brenda, slipped the spoon from her mouth. "What is it, sweetie? Did you eat your ice cream too fast?" She reached for it but had no more success at grabbing it than I had.

Daniel shook his head, and scooped up another bite. Apparently what ever was ailing him hadn't affected his ability to down ice cream.

Brenda lowered herself so she could look Daniel straight in the face. "You said sick, kiddo. Are you sick?"

"No."

"Maybe he meant sick as in good," I offered. "You know, "That car is sick!' Is that it, little buddy?"

This time he looked at me like my brains had just run out of my ears. "No."

Brenda took a deep breath. "You know, sweetheart, you can be real hard to follow sometimes. What did you mean when you said sick?"

He nodded across the room. That wasn't much help. There were several hundred people milling around. "Him. He's sick. Bad."

I still don't understand why Daniel does things like this. We know he sees what the rest of us can't. He sees beings from another world. I believe they're angels and that ability has helped us many times. The problem was, Daniel did very little talkin' about what he saw. Sometimes, Daniel would string several sentences together and for him that was being a chatterbox. Other times he did was he was doing then: one or two words at a time. Frustrating enough to make a Baptist preacher swear.

"What man?" Brenda prompted.

Another frown from Daniel. At times he acted like the smartest person in the room, the kind of smart person lesser brains frustrated.

He pointed with his spoon. I followed his point and saw the professor talking to Allen Krone by the models. Apparently, Krone hadn't been able to escape. My gut wadded up.

"The professor?" I meant my words to be more than a whisper but that was all I could muster.

"No. Him. Krone."

He pronounced Krone as "Croony."

I felt joy. I felt relief. Then I felt guilty.

"Allen Krone? The man we were talking to a few

minutes ago?" Brenda was showing remarkable patience. She always did with Daniel. I sometimes think that's why she has so little patience with the rest of us. Daniel uses it all up.

Daniel nodded. "Bad sick." He walked away, bowl of ice cream in hand.

Brenda rose. "Maybe this is more than a retirement party."

"You mean like a going away party?" Andi said. "A final going away party?"

"Makes sense." Andi kept her eyes on Allen Krone. "You know, I thought I caught a yellow cast to his skin, but the lighting in this building is a little weird. Makes it hard to be certain about colors."

"That's sad." I meant it. I know we all check out of this life at some point, but knowing that doesn't make it easier.

"I have an idea," Andi said.

It must have been a good idea because she set her cake down and walked away. Brenda did the same with her bowl. I didn't have anything to set down so I just followed Andi.

Twenty steps later we were standing in a small maze of five-foot high partitions. They were covered with photos of Allen Krone through the years. Krone graduating architecture school; Krone at a drafting table with a drawing on the board; Krone at a computer, a floor plan on the monitor; Krone wearing a white hardhat standing in front of a large building under construction. There were wedding photos, and pictures of him shaking hands with important people from around the world.

"Do you see it?" Andi asked.

"See what?" I guess that answered her question.

"Krone used to be a lot heavier." Andi kept moving from photo to photo. "Not fat. He looks fit in the pictures."

"He's not young, you know." Brenda leaned close to one of the displays.

"He's just sixty, Brenda," Andi said. "The same age as Dr. McKinney."

I recalled Daniel's little joke about the professor being ancient.

Andi nodded. "I think Daniel is right. Then again, he's always right. Cryptic, but always right."

"Ah, I found you." The professor walked over. "Remarkable man, that Krone. His ability to see in three dimensions and translate those ideas to a set of two dimensional plans is amazing. Did you know..." He looked at us. "What?"

"Krone is sick," Brenda said. "Maybe terminal."

"Who told you that?" The professor had put on his I'm-ready-to-burst-your-bubble face.

"Daniel." The three answered in unison.

"Daniel is not a doctor. How can he know if Krone is sick?"

We stared at him.

He raised his hand and aimed his palm at us. "Okay, okay, that was stupid of me. Did he have anything else to say?"

Andi answered. "No. He just said that Krone was sick and then said it was bad." Look at the photos. He looks very different in his pictures, even the ones dated from just a year ago."

The professor, being the professor, did just that. He studied the photos like Sherlock Holmes studying a crime scene. Finally, he looked at us. There was a good deal of sadness in his eyes. "Maybe cancer. Maybe a degenerative muscular disorder. Maybe... No sense guessing. It doesn't change anything." He sighed. "I thought there was a sadness about him. He knows that his retirement will be short—"

There was a rumble. It came through the floor. It spread to the windows. There were screams and shouts.

The lights flickered then went out.

The building swayed. It moved so much I expected the skyscraper to break in half. I seized Andi by the arm to steady her and did the same to Brenda. The professor went down on his keister. The partitions around began to dance and slide on their chrome feet.

"Daniel!" Brenda's shout wasn't loud enough to

defeat the noise of the rattling building.

"Wait!" I held her tight. "Wait!"

Thirty seconds later, the shaking stopped. Emergency lights filled the open space with dim light. The decorative blue light we had first seen when we arrived was gone.

"Andi, check on the professor." I let her go. "Come on Brenda."

We emerged from the partition maze into the open area. People littered the floor. Most were struggling to their feet. I heard the word "earthquake" a dozen times. I scanned the fallen crowd. Maybe I should have been concerned about injuries but at the moment I could only think of Daniel.

"Let's split up. I'll go—"

"I see him." Brenda pointed. "By the window."

There he was, still on his feet, or maybe he just got up. It didn't matter. We raced to him, stepping around, and on a few occasions stepping over, people on the floor.

Daniel was inches from the window, his bowl of ice cream rested on the floor next to him. Chocolate was spattered on the carpet, window, and Daniel's pants' leg If that window had shattered during the earthquake—I still can't think about it. What I could think about was an aftershock.

Daniel gazed out the window.

Then began to scream like a siren.

I charged forward, hoping no one got in my way.

No one did.

I scooped Daniel up and hugged him tight. I barely glanced out the window, but even that set my teeth on edge. I ignored what I thought I saw and, at a slower pace moved away from the glass wall. I hadn't made it more than six feet when Brenda reached me.

"Let me have him."

"In a sec. Let's get someplace safer."

She started to argue but saw the wisdom in waiting a few moments. We walked around people, most of whom were now on their feet. Some of the women were crying. Some of the men were swearing. To be fair, a good number of women were swearing too.

I found a spot devoid of crowds and released Daniel to Brenda. She was on the verge of tears. If you knew Brenda the way I do, and if you've faced danger with her the way I have, then that statement would surprise you. She took Daniel in her arms as if she would never let go.

"Hey, buddy." I began to look him over, best I could. "That was kinda scary, huh." I kept my voice calm. He had stopped screaming but he hadn't stopped staring at the window. "Are you hurt? Did you fall during the earthquake?"

He shook his head.

"You sure. No bruises. No ouches?"

When I said "ouches" he looked at me like I had lost my mind. Sometimes I think that ten-year-old is older than me.

"Is he okay?" The professor joined us. Andi was with

him.

"I think so," I said. "I can't find anything wrong but he got a good scare."

"We all got a good scare." The professor moved closer to Daniel. I noticed he limped.

"Are you hurt, Professor?"

He waved me off. "I bruised a butt cheek."

Then I heard the sweetest sound I've ever heard. In the middle of all the confusion, I heard Daniel giggle.

"Butt cheek." He giggled again. The sound of it was better than music. "He said 'butt cheek.'"

Andi stepped to Brenda. The two bickered constantly but at this moment, all voices were quiet. Andi wrapped her arms around Brenda and Daniel. Where Brenda was holding back tears, Andi let them flow.

The professor and I helped people to their feet and checked on injuries. There was nothing serious, although the professor wasn't alone with his butt cheek injury.

Then I heard a man's voice: strong, loud, and filled with terror-laced obscenities. I've spent a lot of time on a football field so I've heard everything, but never in such rapid order.

I saw the man near the window.

He was staring out and down.

He vomited.

Chapter 5

SOMETHIN' AIN'T RIGHT

THE MAN'S OUTBURST quieted the crowd for a few moments. No one approached. I can't blame them. For a few moments there was a hush. I glanced at my friends. All the excitement and my fear for Daniel's safety had forced the glimpse I had out the window from my brain. Now it was trying to worm its way forward.

"Tank, where are you going?" Andi sounded terrified. That just meant she was like the rest of us.

"Stay here."

"Tank?"

"Stay here—please."

I worked my way through guests. It was like pushing through a forest of small trees. I lost sight of the man at the window but reacquired him a few steps later. He had turned. His mouth moved as if he expected words to come out, but apparently he had run dry. The smell of the vomit filled the air. The stain of it clung to the front of his tux.

Unable to speak, he pointed out the window. Out and down.

"Take it easy, sir." I tried to sound calm and in control. I never was a very good actor. "Maybe you should step away from the window."

"L-l-l…"

"Easy, buddy. We'll get through this. We just gotta stay calm and focused. We all need each other now." I kept a slow pace toward him.

"L-lo-lo."

I smiled and motioned for him to walk toward me. He turned his back to the window, then to me. "Look!"

I did and my mind started to overheat. Now *I* felt like vomiting, but I'm pretty sure that a dozen other people with sensitive stomachs might follow my lead. So I kept my last meal down.

And I gazed out and down.

Out and down almost fifty floors to the street below, except I couldn't see the street. Instead, I saw a fog. There was no way for me to be accurate about my guess, but the fog looked to cap out at just about five feet above the street. I came to that conclusion because hundreds of people had spilled from surrounding buildings and into the streets. I don't know how good an idea that is after an earthquake but I didn't have any better ideas.

The fog was everywhere. I couldn't see cars, just the heads of a few people and the noggin tops of a few shorter people.

Then I saw why the man had cursed. I realized what made him empty his stomach. Somethin' was moving in the fog and it wasn't even close to being human.

What people I could see were running in different directions. They seemed to be running in slow motion. One man—I knew he was tall because I could see his shoulders. He wore some kinda baseball style cap. He was doing his best to run up the street. As he ran he looked over his shoulder. I don't know what he was seeing but it had him scared. Really scared.

Ten steps into his sprint something broke the surface like a shark in the ocean. I couldn't see it clearly. Fifty floors is something like five or six hundred feet. What I was looking at didn't seem large but I had a feeling it was deadly.

It was.

The thing moved through the fog with ease. It seemed to be swimming. Ridiculous I know but I've become used to seeing and believing the ridiculous.

I do know one thing: what I was seeing wasn't human. People say there ain't no such thing as monsters, but tell that to a seal being chased by a killer whale. Monster is in the eye of the beholder and I was seeing something monstrous.

And it wasn't alone. Another breached the surface of the fog, then another. Before I could draw a deep breath they caught the tall man with the cap. He went down, replaced by a mist of red.

My knees threatened to betray me. I rested a hand on the glass, bent forward and wished for amnesia. "Dear God. My dear Jesus." I'm the religious one of our group so those words were prayer. If not for them I might have used the same language as my vomit tinged friend.

Inhale. Exhale. Inhale. Slowly. Slowly. Exhale. I forced my heart to slow. I resisted the urge to scream like a girl scout. I was determined not to lose control. I couldn't let others see that. Most of all I couldn't let Daniel see it.

I straightened. "Professor. I need to show you something."

"We're coming."

"No! Just you." I turned. "Leave the girls behind." My voice came out an octave higher.

"But Tank—" Andi began.

"I said, no!"

That was a first. I had never snapped at Andi, or any of the others. Odd what watching people die could do to a man.

"Tank, what is it?" The professor looked shook.

I couldn't put enough syllables together to make words so I nodded to the window. The professor annoys me a great deal but once you get past his arrogance, he's an okay guy. I hated doing this to him.

"I'm not going to like this, am I, Tank."

"No, sir. I'm sorry."

He exhaled noisily. I couldn't help noticing the unblinking eyes fixed on us. No one spoke. No one moved. It was group-wide paralysis. Wives hung onto husbands, dates hung onto each other. All of them were looking at us. Better they look at us than what was on the street.

The professor, always calm, always logical, always with a straight back and packing lots of extra superiority forced himself to gaze into the darkness, lit only by moon light.

He stood as rigid as a goal post. His breathing slowed. His back bent. His hands shook. He sniffed like a person about to burst into tears.

Then came a whisper. "Those poor souls. Horrid."

I slipped to his side and watched the carnage below. I saw another man go down and the red smear rise where he had been. Then a woman. Then several young women, best I could tell, then—dear God—a parent with a child on his shoulders.

Both—

I closed my eyes. After everything I had seen. After the dangers we have faced as a team. After all the impossible weirdness, this terrified me more.

"Steady on, lad," the professor whispered. "Everyone here is taking their lead from us. We lose it; they lose it. Understand."

"Yep. I know. I was going to say the same thing."

The professor nodded. "You might have to remind me."

A familiar voice came from my left. Allen Krone was there. "Not to worry, gentlemen. This building is designed to withstand earthquakes. It has the latest features. We're safe here. However, it might be good if you backed away from—"

His gaze shifted from us to the street.

I caught him before he hit the floor.

In two beats of my heart two others joined us. One was an African-American woman with salt-and-pepper hair cut so close to her scalp she was an eighth of an inch from bald. Her features were sharp. To tell the truth, she was stunning, even at middle-age. I recognized Ebony Watt from the pictures Andi showed us in the limo.

The second person was Jonathan Waterridge, Krone's other partner. He approached quickly but calmly. He didn't strike me as a man prone to panic. A good quality right now. Waterridge took Krone's other arm. "What is it Allen?"

"I'm fine, Jon. Just…um…" He pointed at the window.

"Can you stand?" Waterridge looked Krone up and down like a doctor with X-ray eyes.

Krone nodded. "I'm okay, now." His voice sounded stronger.

Waterridge slowly released Krone's other arm and seeing that his partner wasn't going to do a header, moved to the window. Both looked out, then down. Neither reacted.

"The fog?" Waterridge asked.

I answered for him. "Yes."

Waterridge and Watt exchanged glances then turned their attention back to us.

"I don't get it," Watt said. I detected a slight accent in her voice. "It's just fog."

I caught the professor staring at me. He went to the window for another look. I was happy to stay where I was and serve as Krone prop.

Waterridge stepped back to Krone. "I thought maybe there was damage from the earthquake, bodies in the street, fires, something, but all I see is fog."

Krone spoke in hushed tones. "There are things in the fog. I saw them. Creatures."

"Creatures?" Waterridge looked at me. "We need to get Mr. Krone a chair. He needs to rest."

I recognized the tone. I hear it each time I'm forced to tell someone what our team deals with: disbelief. "I saw them too. So did the professor."

The professor said nothing. He kept his gaze glued to the sights below.

"Tell them, Dr. McKinney. They'll believe you."

The professor turned. "Tank. The fog is rising."

Not what I wanted to hear.

EBONY WATT AND Janice Krone, who seemed to appear from nowhere, helped me get Krone to a chair. Waterridge decided the guests needed a little encouragement.

"Ladies and gentleman," he said, "thank you for your calm and courageous response. It's been quite an evening. First let me assure you, you are in a safe place. This building not only meets the most rigid earthquake standards, it exceeds them. You are safe here."

"But we should leave, right?" some woman in the crowd said.

"No, not yet. As you can tell, we're on emergency power. Buildings this size have only one elevator that can operate on emergency power. I will check to see if the generator is working or if the earthquake knocked it off line. Our best way out will be the stairwells, but I suggest we wait for a bit. There will probably be an aftershock soon and you're less likely to get hurt here than trying to walk down nearly fifty floors. Most likely, the power will be back on soon and the elevators will be on line."

"You're sure we're safe here?" This time it was a man's voice, a frightened man's voice. "I felt the building sway."

"Absolutely." Waterridge tucked his hands into his pants pockets like a man without a care in the world. "Not many people know this, but architects and structural engineers design tall buildings to sway. If they didn't sway in strong wind or earthquakes they would experience much more damage. I know it may have felt like more, but the sway was only a couple of feet in each direction. So, swaying is good—even if it feels otherwise.

"That being said, I suggest we stay calm. Help yourself to the food and drink. Not too much on the alcohol just in case we all have to walk down the stairs. It would be bad form to survive an earthquake then break a toe on the exit stairs." That brought a few chuckles.

"For now," Waterridge continued, "I ask that you stay away from the windows. I'm being over cautious, I know, but humor me."

The guy was smooth, I had to give him that.

I LEFT ALLEN Krone in the care of his wife and worked my way to my friends. Brenda still held Daniel. I'm pretty sure it would take a crowbar to loosen her grip. Daniel seemed fine with that.

"What's going on?" Andi kept her voice low. "What did that guy see out there? What did you see? Daniel said something about sharks. Sharks? Really?"

The professor raised a hand. "Easy, Andi. One question at a time."

"Sorry. I'm a little shook. And I don't mean by the earthquake. That didn't help."

I stepped next to her and put my arm around her shoulder. She was trembling.

"Not sharks," the professor said. "Worse." He tried to describe what we saw, toning down the gruesome details, probably for Daniel's benefit.

"Where'd they come from?" Brenda almost sounded like her old self. No doubt, she would be telling each of us where to get off soon. I looked forward to that.

"I don't know." The professor said.

"I don't want to know," I said. "I just want them to go back where they came from."

"So this is why we're here?" Andi looked around. "It must be."

"How are we gonna do that?" Brenda said. "If I heard right, we ain't going down there and start exchanging punches with those things."

"I have no idea," the professor said. "I'm open to creative thoughts."

No one had any.

The building began to shake again.

A RISING FOG

THE GUESTS HAD clumped into small groups.
Loud laughter had been replaced with mumbles and
occasionally nervous chuckles. Some ate. Some paced.
Some stood around looking lost. For the first half-
hour nearly everyone pulled out their smartphones
and pressed them into service, except there was no
service. No phone calls. No texts. No e-mail. No
Internet. I'll admit it, I did the same thing as did the
professor, Andi, and Brenda.

Mr. Waterridge returned and told everyone that he
had used a landline to reach fire and rescue. "They
suggest we wait here. Apparently it's a little confusing
at ground level."

A little confusing? After what I had seen of the
murderous things in the fog it was no problem
believing there might be a bit of confusion. The
horrible sights returned and my fear elevated a good
bit. I felt just as sick now as when I first saw the
monstrosities mowing down people in the street.

A thin woman stepped forward. "Our cell phones
still don't work. Can we use the landline to call our

families? They'll be worried and we're worried about them."

Waterridge's face showed great compassion and understanding. It also tipped me off to the answer.

"I wish you could. I understand the problem but I'm afraid the phone line went dead just before I finished the call. I'm sure it will be up in no time. The best thing for us to do now is be patient. I'm sure we'll all be headed home soon."

I wasn't so sure. From the professor's expression, he wasn't convinced either. The girls didn't have to say anything for me to know they were carrying a load of doubt. We had seen too much in the past to know that all this would blow over if we just sat tight. At least Brenda had set Daniel down. He's ten, a bit big to be held like a toddler.

While Waterridge continued to talk, the professor motioned with his head for me to follow him. I did but I didn't like where he was leading me. He made for the windows. Really? I have to look down there again? I kept my fears to myself. I'm supposed to be the macho guy of the group but my machismo was paper thin.

"What do you see, Tank?"

Now you know why I call him the professor. Okay, he was a professor, that's the big reason, but if you hang with the guy you soon learn that he loves to teach and test. He always has an opinion, and wants to make sure we know he's the one with the brains.

"I see fog. It's what I don't see that scares me. Those things below the top surface of the fog."

"I know what you mean." He shuddered. I don't think I've ever seen him shudder. "That, however, is not what I'm getting at, Tank. Look again."

Something the professor said to me came back. It had been a stab in the heart the first time, but I was focused on holding up Mr. Krone. "The fog is rising, just like you said."

"It's rising fast."

Since I couldn't see the street below the best I could do is guess at how much the stuff had risen. When I first looked out the window, I could see the heads of pedestrians. Sometimes it was just the top of their heads, but with taller people I could see all the way to their shoulders. I couldn't see that now. Of course, for all I knew, the fog-monsters might have eaten all the people below. Now, I could see nothing but the churning fog. No trucks. No busses. No tall vehicles at all.

"I can't be sure," I said, "but I'm guessin' the fog is up to the forth or fifth floor."

"That's my estimation too."

As we watched, several of the creatures broke the surface, their heads swiveling from side to side. Then they looked up."

"They're looking at us, Professor."

"Maybe. I doubt they can see us."

They began to move in a circle, like sharks. The sight of that poured ice-water down my spine. Despite the professor's doubt, I felt sure those things were sizing us up. A few moments later, the creatures disappeared below the surface again.

The professor turned and I followed him away from the windows and the unwanted view they provided. We had moved only a few steps when I saw Mr. Krone motioning for us to come to where he was seated. His wife Janice stood by his side. I didn't have to be a mind reader to know how frightened she was.

When we reached him, I dropped to a knee to better look him in the eyes. There was still a keen intelligence there. If Daniel was right—what am I saying—Daniel is always right. The kid said Krone was sick. It wasn't obvious. I doubt most people in the room knew. That's probably as Krone wanted it.

I gave a little smile to our host. "How you doin', Mr. Krone?"

"Call me, Allen."

"Only if you call me, Tank."

"I'm fine."

I looked at Janice. It's been my experience that spouses are more truthful about the health of their partners. She cocked her head. I took that to mean she wasn't in full agreement.

Krone rose from the chair. I was on my feet a second later. "You should rest."

"Nonsense. I don't want my guests to worry unduly." He stretched his back and wobbled an inch or two. It took a lot of will power for me not to seize his arm. He steadied.

"What did you see? Just now, I mean."

We didn't answer at first.

"I saw you at the window. I'm pretty good at reading body language. Unless I miss my guess, you saw something that made you...uncomfortable."

Uncomfortable. That was an understatement. Still, we said nothing.

"Okay, gentlemen. I saw those things too. In fact, I keep seeing it in my head, so I'm not going to be shocked by talk of monsters and whatever that fog is. You're in my building. You owe me the honor of the truth."

The professor pressed his lips into a line and

looked at Janice.

"My wife can take it. Information is better than ignorance. Now tell me what you saw."

"The fog is rising, sir. Before we could see almost to street level. The fog was, maybe, five feet above grade. I make it to be up to about the fourth floor now."

"And it's still rising?"

"Yes." The professor shifted his weight. "I would have to observe it over time to guess at the rate of its climb but it is significant."

Krone nodded, then lowered his head like a man deep in thought. "Fog can get pretty high, and I doubt this is ordinary fog. Creatures can swim in the stuff. That's not normal."

"I need to ask a question if I may, sir." The professor kept his eyes on the man.

"Ask it."

"The stairwells—could the fog get into them?"

Krone nodded. Stairwells are not airtight. There needs to be an exchange of air, so yes, fog could seep in at the base of the exit doors at street level."

"What about the floors below grade."

"Yes. We have to assume that if the fog was at street level, and we know it was, that it could have poured into the parking floors below the building."

"That means the parking floors could be teeming with those things." I thought it worth mentioning.

"Yes," Krone said, "but we're asking the wrong question. The question isn't whether or not the fog can get in, but whether or not the creatures can get in."

"I think they need the fog." The professor put his hands behind his back striking a relaxed pose I know he didn't feel. "The few times I've seen the creatures stick their heads above the fog they soon submerged again. If submerged is the right word."

"Works for me," I said.

"The fog is like water is to fish."

I could see the professor's point. "So what happens if the fog rises to the floor we're on?"

"They still have to get in. They can't fit under the door." Krone spoke without conviction.

"No, Tank, they can't but they have hands. Hands with claws. At least the best I can tell." This time it was the professor who lowered his head in thought. "Mr. Krone—Allen—no one knows more about this building than you and your partners. Is there any way those things can get into the building?"

Krone shook his head then stopped abruptly as if a thought had slammed into his head. "I'm just thinking aloud here. Let's assume they can go wherever the fog goes. The higher the fog, the higher they can move. That would have to be true on the inside of the building too." He fell silent. "If I were them, I'd open the doors to the stairwells, but I'd find away to open the doors to the elevators in the parking structure. Fog would pour in. If the cab is there, they could tear out the ceiling. The fog would climb the shaft at the same rate it's climbing outside the building."

I wasn't enjoying this conversation. A motion to my left grabbed my attention. It was Andi. She had Daniel with her. She stepped forward and smiled at Krone. "Excuse me. May I steal my two friends away for a little while?"

The professor didn't appreciate the interruption. He hated interruptions. "Andi, we're in the middle of a conversation."

She gave him a look that said, "Shut up and come with me." That's what I got out of it. Apparently, the professor got the same message. We put some distance between us and anyone else.

"This better be good, Andi. We're in a life and death situation here."

"Ya think?" She closed her eyes and took a deep breath. "There's something you need to see."

"If you mean outside—"

"I don't," she snapped. "Follow me."

Andi is a nice person. I think the world of her. She has skills no one else has, so when I hear anger in her voice, I get confused. Then I get afraid. She started for the back of the cavernous room.

"Where are we going?" the professor asked. At least he wasn't resisting anymore.

"The lady's restroom."

"Well, of course." The professor cut his eyes my way. I chose to remain silent.

The restrooms were along the back wall. The only wall without windows. We stopped a few feet from the door to the restroom. A similar door nearby was marked for men.

"Brenda went missing while you two were taking in the sights. She left Daniel with me. She had that odd look she gets sometimes. When she didn't return, I got worried, so I went searching. I found her in the restroom."

"She's been known to use bathrooms before." The professor thought he was being cute, but Andi disagreed. "Once, just for once, old man, stop trying to prove what a jerk you can be."

"Old man?"

"Ancient," Daniel said.

If carnivorous creatures swimming in a fog hadn't already put me on the razor's edge, Andi's behavior would have done it. Andi had been the professor's assistant for a good long time and no one knew him better. She normally showed great respect. Something had pushed Andi beyond her normal behavior.

The professor opened his mouth then closed it. I was thankful for that.

"As I was saying. She disappeared. I went looking. I found her in here. She's been at it again."

Andi turned and plowed into the lady's restroom, holding the door open for us. Daniel walked in with her. I hesitated. I mean, it was the girl's bathroom after all. Andi stared at me. Andi narrowed her eyes. Andi tapped a foot. I walked in, the professor right behind me.

This was awkward. I have to admit that I've never been in the lady's room. Never had need to be. Its size surprised me. Two emergency lights blazed from opposite corners. The light was harsh but needed.

Andi led us past a set of stalls then stopped. There was Brenda. Sitting on the tile floor staring at the white tile on the wall. She had hiked up her evening gown enough to allow her to sit on the floor. It wasn't a good look for her.

As I said earlier, Brenda is a tattoo artist. And I mean a real artist. We all have our "sometimes" gifts. Andi sees and sorts patterns like a computer; the professor denies any special skills but he does some pretty special thinking; I heal people—sometimes, it's very hit and miss. I don't know why. Yes, I've been thinking about having a go at healing Mr. Krone but I've had monsters on the mind. Brenda draws things.

When the urge comes over her she has to put the images in her brain on paper, or if she's doing a tattoo, ink it into someone's skin. That has led to some interesting conversations.

The thing with Brenda's spontaneous drawings is that they usually don't make sense until later, but she's never wrong.

Never.

Which is why her sketch terrified me. Using a magic marker, she had drawn a spot on image of the creatures showing detail we couldn't see from our position. She also sketched several human figures, all half eaten. It was sickening, but not as sickening as the third image.

"Oh, Tank." The professor made the connection.

The third image stung just to look at it. It was me. On the floor of some building. My chest had been ripped open and my eyes were gone. Three of the creatures squatted around me—feasting on my organs.

I no longer cared that I was in the lady's room.

Brenda began to weep. Brenda never weeps.

A ROOM WITH A TERRIFYING VIEW

I SAT ON the floor next to Brenda and gently took the Magic Marker from her hand. She didn't resist. Brenda is as hard as nails. I know that's a cliché, but the words could be chiseled on her tombstone. She doesn't talk about her child hood but I know enough to wonder how she turned out as wonderful as she is. She grew up street smart and with fierceness that could cower a charging rhino. She's also, despite all her talk and threats, a deep, loving soul.

I may just be a college-age kid but I know a little about people. Someone as heartbroken as Brenda didn't need words of comfort. She needed an arm around her shoulder and I had a big arm that could do the job, so I used it.

Daniel moved close and sat on the other side of Brenda. He scooted close enough that his little shoulder touched her arm. He said nothing.

No one said anything.

The professor, who could ruin any moment, lowered himself to the floor next to me. A moment later, Andi did the same next to Daniel. There we were, five silent, shaken, confused, and frightened friends sitting on the floor of the lady's bathroom doing our best not to look at Brenda's wall art.

A few minutes later, I took another look. There I was, dead and being devoured. I wished Brenda had not been such a good artist. Based on Brenda's earlier success, it looks like I was going to die and die badly.

Then the building shook again.

TEN MINUTES OR so later, we walked from the bathroom—a line of two men, two women, and a boy. In any other circumstance, people would have thought it strange. If they did now, they didn't say so. The crowd had separated into small clumps of people. Some stood as couples; others in small gatherings of four or so.

I spied the mayor in the middle of the room trying for all he was worth to get his cell phone to work. Those with him did the same. That made sense. He was the mayor of a major city after all—a city that had experience a powerful earthquake and several bone rattling aftershocks. Oh, and a city that had been invaded by killer creatures who swam through fog: a fog that was rising every minute.

I also couldn't help noticing that more and more people had gathered around the bar. That didn't seem very wise. The professor noticed it too.

"Fools. Don't they know they need to keep their wits sharp at a time like this?"

"Their scared out of their minds." Andi had her eyes fixed on those knocking back hard liquor.

"That's no excuse, Andi. If they get themselves drunk, they will become a danger to others and themselves." The professor spotted Ebony Watt and her husband. "I'm gonna have a word with her. Maybe she can close the bar down."

I let that be his problem. I turned to Andi and Brenda, "I'm gonna check on the fog."

"I'll stay with Brenda and Daniel." Andi placed a hand on Brenda shoulder. To Brenda's credit, she was recovering nicely—considering.

I hadn't been at the window a full minute when the professor joined me. "Ms. Watt is shutting the bar down. I like her. Strong in the face of adversity."

"That's what I admire about you and the rest of the team."

"You know, Tank, Brenda isn't always right."

"Name a time when she wasn't."

He looked out the window. "She does a lot of drawing and tattoo work. Not all of those were predictions."

"I appreciate what you're doing, Professor. I really do, but you know there's a difference. You saw her. When was the last time you saw Brenda that emotional?"

"Tank—"

"It's okay, Professor. You know about my faith. You were a Catholic priest; you know what Christians of all denominations believe about death. I'm not afraid to die. Death is just a promotion."

I waited for his usual chatter about faith being a myth and how he gave it all up to embrace reason and logic. It never came. I guess there was enough priest left in him to know not to belittle a dying man's faith.

Still, he squirmed. I let him off the hook. "The fog is rising faster. I figure it's halfway up the building. I can see the fog creatures more clearly now. Can't say I like it any."

"We have to figure something out, Tank. We can't let all these people die. We can't let those things win."

"You got that right, old man." It was Brenda and she sounded like Brenda. Andi stood next to her.

The professor closed his eyes and sighed. "I'm not an old man, Barnick."

"Ancient." Daniel was by her side. This time he didn't lose control but I could tell he'd rather be someplace else. I understood the feeling.

The professor eyed the boy and tried to look angry but the smile on his face defused the act. "Should he be here?"

"It was his idea, Professor." A second later she added. "And by the way. Thanks."

Andi fidgeted. "I feel useless."

"Feelings are useless, Andi. You know that. We have to approach this with logic."

"Shut up, McKinney," Brenda snapped. Man it was good to have her back.

Andi continued as if the exchange hadn't happened. "I can't make sense of things. I'm looking for patterns, things out of the ordinary."

"That's pretty far from ordinary." Brenda pointed out the window at the creature infested fog.

"I'm going to the roof," I said.

"Why?" the professor asked.

"To see more. To get a better idea how fast the fog is climbing. I can lean over the edge and see how high the fog is. We might be dealing with other factors."

There was a moment of silence, which the professor broke. "Who are you and what have you done with Tank?"

"Yeah, what he said." Brenda's tone had returned to normal.

Andi wasn't going to be outdone. "I'm going with you and don't tell me no. You don't have the authority."

The professor cleared his throat. "Me too. We also need to see if the fog is rising in the stairwell."

I thought that was a good idea.

We crossed paths with Allen Krone who was looking stronger. I asked if the stairwell went all the way to the roof. He said it did. I then mentioned our plan. Turns out, that was a bad idea. He insisted on going. I told him that it wasn't advisable. Janice, his wife, agreed with me. The professor backed me up. So did Andi. Four against one. I figured that would end the matter but Krone countered with, "It's my building." No need to go into what words he used to spice up that statement. Bottom line, he was going with us.

We approached the stairwell individually hoping not to alert the crowd that we were stepping out for a few minutes. We gathered near the door and chatted for a few moments then slipped from the room.

The space was dim, lit from above by emergency lights. I could see light glowing down the stairs too. I wanted to see if the fog had come up the stairs but decided we should go to the roof first.

We moved up the stairs slowly but it was still a tad too fast for Krone. I tried to talk him into going back. He had no interest in that and said so. We were four people climbing steps to who knows what. Still it felt good to be doing something more than standing around.

Krone stopped to rest a coupla times but only for a few moments. Each time, I stood beside him and put an arm around his shoulders. Partly to comfort him; mostly in hopes that my healing gift, sporadic as it is, might kick in.

Nothing. I'm thankful to God for the few people that I've healed—there have only been a handful (a small handful at that)—but I get frustrated with it. What good is it to have a healing gift if you can't use it when you need to? I've had these thoughts before and when I do I comfort myself with the knowledge that Brenda's gift is on-again-off-again. Same is true for Andi. Her mind is always sharp and seeing things the rest of us don't, but she doesn't see patterns in everything everyday. Still, her ability seems to be there when she needs it.

Fortunately, we started on the top floor so the roof was only one full flight of stairs away. When we reached the upper landing, I saw a metal door. It bore a plastic plaque telling us this was the roof access. FOR USE IN EMERGENCIES ONLY.

I think our situation qualified.

THE NIGHT AIR was cool but I couldn't detect even a hint of a breeze. We propped the door open to make sure it couldn't lock behind us. We were probably being paranoid, but paranoia was understandable today.

I looked around. The roof was flat and covered with something that looked like a black rubber flooring. Concrete paths led in several directions. One led to roof mounted machinery, another to what looked like small rooms, and one to the edge of the building. The same kind of concrete walk ran the perimeter of the building. I assumed the walkways were there to keep maintenance people from walking on the rubber-like surface. Krone confirmed my suspicions. He then pointed out a few details.

"The walkway runs around the edge of the building. It's there for the window cleaners." He pointed to a short wall at the edge of the building. There are anchors to support davits—small crane-like devices—along the parapet. The crews place the davits where they need them. It allows them to swing a window cleaner's platform over the edge of the building."

He pointed to some large mechanical equipment. Much of the HVAC equipment is up here. Those small buildings you see are elevator equipment rooms."

"You mean like pulleys and stuff?" I asked.

"Yes, and more. This building is too tall to use hydraulic elevators so we use an electric system. The cars are pulled up and lowered on cables."

It was all interesting and a great way to stall, but the time had come to do what we came for. I moved to the edge of the building until I was standing next to the wall Krone had called a parapet.

The light up here came from emergency lights and a veiled moon. I could see more stars than I expected in the downtown area of a major city. With the city lights out, there was almost no light pollution.

Fog reached as far as I could see in the dark city. I remembered the people on the streets we had seen from the limo: the partiers, show-goers, business people, and homeless. I tried not to think how many were now dead or how they died.

The professor saw the same thing and groaned. I leaned over the parapet and studied the teeming fog. Now and again, one of those things would poke its head up and each time the sight of its ugly face turned my stomach. Maggots looked better.

"I can barely see the green band," Andi said. "The fog must be higher than the thirteenth floor."

Krone nodded. "I'd estimate the fog is up to the twenty-fifth floor."

"So half way, then." It seemed higher to me.

"More than halfway, Tank," the professor said. "Remember, only forty-eight floors are above grade."

"That doesn't make me feel any better."

As we watched, the fog rose another few feet. It was definitely growing faster, bringing death with it.

The city was dark everywhere except the area around us—about two blocks.

"I'm gonna take a lap." I walked next to the parapet, my gaze shifting from the fog below to darkness everywhere else. As I walked west I noticed I couldn't see the waters of the bay. Even the ocean wore a blanket of fog. I'll confess, I was losing heart, which is sad, since I'm supposed to be the optimist of the group.

I followed the concrete path around the edge of the building. I could hear the others behind me. The spoke on occasion, but barely above a whisper. They were as stunned as I was.

Behind the building was a gap. Another building, dark as a tomb stood on the other side of the gap. The fog was as high here as it was at the front of the building. Why wouldn't it be? It was fog.

"Alley," Krone said. "There's a narrow alley behind the building. If memory serves it's about twenty feet wide."

Good to know, but useless. I had hoped there was a back way out, a place without the fog. It was a ridiculous hope, but then this whole thing was ridiculous.

We made our way back to where we started. "We're stuck," I said. I studied the fog more intently. A creature popped his grotesque head up and stared at me. The he pointed at me. It's probably my imagination, but for a moment I thought he smiled.

Andi gasped. I snapped my head around and saw here staring across the street at the building opposite the one we were on. Like Krone's building it was tall, but three or four stories shorter. It looked fairly new. Like many buildings in San Diego it looked made of glass.

The lights had gone on. Not emergency lights. All the lights in it. I looked at other buildings. All dark. I leaned over the parapet and looked down the side of our structure. Still dark.

"What's going on—" Then I saw. Dear Lord, I didn't want to see. The lights inside the building illuminated everything but all I could see was fog. Fog inside the building. And in the fog, people running, and unpeople swimming—attacking. Blood painted the windows.

I couldn't watch.

"Did you see?" The professor said.

"We all saw, Professor. Horrible."

Andi covered her mouth. "I'm going to be sick."

"I meant the fog. The fog inside the building. It's at a higher level than the fog outside. That means…"

He didn't finish and I'm glad. We knew what it meant.

The lights across the street flickered then winked out. We couldn't see inside. That was the only blessing of the moment.

Then we heard a scream. No, not "a" scream; several screams. I sprinted to the stairwell. The professor was close behind.

SCREAMS FROM A STAIRWELL

I POUNDED DOWN the stairs and rounded the middle landing. There were too many things to see. My brain quivered. First I noticed a half dozen people standing on the landing by the door to the floor we had been on most of the night. It looked like they were cons making a prison break. My guess was they saw the slaughter across the street and panicked.

Then I saw several more people standing on the first flight of stairs going down. They stopped in mid step, no doubt frozen by the screams of those who had gone before.

I saw one other thing: Brenda, sitting half on the landing half on the first step down. Daniel was in her arms. He was shaking.

"Back into the room!" My voice echoed in the stairwell.

Those on the platform turned and stared at me. I descended the remaining steps. No one had moved. "I said, get back in the room."

One guy, a six-footer in his thirties sneered at me. He should see what linemen do. "Who do you think you are to give orders?" He poked me in the chest with his index finger. At the moment I wasn't sure if he was brave or stupid. It didn't matter. I had to put an end to the panic and I could only think of one thing to do, so I did it.

I seized the front of his dress shirt, just above his vest, pulled forward and, when he tried to resist my pull, pushed back and up pinning him against the door jamb.

"Okay, mister. Here's the deal. You're scared. I'm scared. The difference is I'm younger, stronger, and twice your size. Am I getting through to you?"

He nodded.

"Good. I'm trying to help. Don't…" I lifted him another two inches, "get in my way. We good?"

"Y-yes."

I dropped him and took a deep breath.

"Everyone, please go in the room. Right now it's the safest place to be. There's nothing but death down these stairs."

One by one they filed back into the room until only Brenda and Daniel were left. I squatted next to them. "You okay?"

"They went nuts. They saw the lights go on the building across the street. They cheered and moved to the windows. Then the slaughter began. They lost it, Cowboy. I mean they went bug nuts, and made a run for the stairwell." She grimaced. Daniel tried to stop them but they knocked him down. I had to get him to safety but they kept pushing toward the door. We got carried along. I was afraid they were gonna trample us. If you hadn't—"

"That part is over," I said. "Are you hurt?"

"My leg is banged up. Knee cap. I think its broken."

"Let me have a look." The professor inched by me onto the stair just below Brenda. Brenda didn't object. They bicker a lot, but I have no doubt either would lay down their life for the other.

"It hurts here?" He pressed the area just below her knee cap. Her yelp was enough of an answer. He studied the leg a little longer, pressed a few more spaces but stopped when Brenda smacked him it the shoulder. "Her arm is working."

"So is my fist."

The professor looked at me. "She's right. I think the patella is broken. That's a guess of course." He looked behind him and down the stairwell. He let his eyes linger. "I'd feel safer inside with the others. Not much, but a little."

I lifted Daniel from Brenda's embrace. "Hey, dude. Are you okay?"

"Yes."

"No injuries, broken bones, bruises, missing limbs?"

He smiled. "No."

"I think you may have saved a bunch of lives. Go with Andi, buddy. I'm gonna give this mean ol' woman a hand up."

"Hey," Brenda said. "You heard me tell, the professor my fists were still working."

That's the Brenda I admire so much.

"Help me up," she said.

"Nope." Instead, I scooped her up in my arms. She cringed and swore—something she's really good at. She wrapped her arms around my neck and I carried her into the room.

The expansive room was close to silent. Something was different. I found the professor, Andi, and Daniel standing near the door. The door closed behind me.

"There are less people here," I said to whoever was listening. "How many made it down the stairs?"

Brenda said, "I don't know. Ten, maybe."

"That doesn't' make sense. There's more than ten missing."

"Cowboy...Tank..." Brenda looked me in eyes, her voice was soft but soaked with sadness. "There's more than one emergency staircase."

"Blessed Jesus." I closed my eyes. "Why did I go to the roof?"

Andi laid a hand on my arm. "Because, this is what we do, Tank. This is our calling. To do our best to fix things. Besides, you can't save everyone."

Nice words but not cool enough to extinguish the fire of guilt in my gut.

I waited for the professor to huff as he usually did when any of us talked that way. The huff never came.

Brenda stiffened for a moment and then stared at her injured leg. "Tank, put me down."

"Let me carry you to a chair."

"Put me down, now."

I lowered Brenda until her feet could reach the floor. She wiggled from my arms and stood on both legs. She bent the one with the busted patella. "I'm not sure that's wise."

"Shut up, Cowboy." She tested her leg by bending it as much as her dress would allow. Then she pressed the area just as the professor had. "No pain." She straightened. "It's like nothing happened." She shot forward and hugged me. Then stepped back. "If you tell anyone I just did that I'll deny it."

"You mean…"

"Yep. You healed me."

I shook my head. "Someday I'll get that figured out."

"I'M MISSING SOMETHING," Andi said. The professor and I were pacing the room with her. Andi does some of her best thinking on her feet. "I'm missing something. I'm missing something."

Yes, she was being redundant but telling her that wouldn't help anything. Then she stopped suddenly. I grabbed the professor's elbow. He was lost in his own thoughts.

"What?" I asked Andi.

"Nothing. Probably nothing. Maybe nothing. I need to see Krone." We gathered up the professor and went looking for the architect.

We found him at the bar drinking a coffee. His wife was by his side. He looked worse than before we went on the roof. Janice looked even more concerned.

"Mr. Krone, may we have a moment?" Andi asked.

"You know, the only satisfaction I have at the moment is this: when one of those creatures bites into me, he's gonna get a mouthful of chemicals."

I didn't expect that. "I don't understand, sir," I said.

"Cancer. I know you've been wondering. I've got only a few months to live. Given the circumstances, I may be robbed of those."

"I'm sorry to hear that, sir." I was. Now I really feel bad about my erratic gift of healing. "But this isn't over yet, Mr. Krone."

"Are you sure?" He studied his coffee as if he could read the future in it. "I don't see any way out of this. I know what I saw. I don't believe it, but I know it's real. Does that make sense?"

Andi answered. "Believe it or not, sir, it makes perfect sense. If you knew us better you'd know why." She manufactured a grin. He didn't look up so he missed Andi's brave face.

"Can I join the party?" Brenda and Daniel had been standing a short distance away. She had been testing her newly healed leg. I didn't know how to feel. I was happy for Brenda but felt a truck-load of guilt about Krone.

Krone looked at her then at Daniel. He stretched forward a thin hand and patted Daniel on the head. Daniel, who didn't warm to strangers easily, allowed it.

"You know, I've created mansions, hospitals, and high-rises around the world. I've used my mind and skills to create important buildings but one creation has eluded me." He looked at his wife. "A child. We weren't able to have children."

Tears glistened in Janice's eyes. I could see the depth of their pain.

"No children. No grandchildren." He turned back to his coffee.

I've met depressed people before. The professor has been known to live in the dark from time to time.

But I don't think I've ever watched someone sink deeper and deeper into depression. It was like watching a man drown.

"Mr. Krone," Andi said. "I hurt for you. I know your pain is great, but I need your help."

"There's nothing I can do for you. Nothing I can do for my wife. Nothing I can do for anyone here." Janice touched his arm but kept silent.

"Mr. Krone, I want to—no, I need to ask a few questions. Will you help me?"

"Go ahead, sweetheart." Janice's was voice soggy with concern. "It can't hurt."

It was my turn. "Mr. Krone, you've been very helpful. I know we're still in a bind, but we can't give up. Andi notices things we don't. You can trust her."

The professor said, "Tank is right."

Krone sighed and straightened as if getting ready to exert himself. "What do you want to know."

Andi grinned. "Thank you." She took a deep breath. "When I was on the roof I looked over the edge like everyone with us, and like everyone my attention was fixed on those ugly things swimming in the fog, and the…what happened in the other building. Now it occurs to me that I saw something else. A green glow below the fog."

"The horizontal element." Krone picked up on the fact that we had no idea what he was talking about. "It's part of the exterior design, like the arched entryway. The bulk of the building is blocky, those elements break up the stark lines of the building. In architecture we call it gingerbread—stuff added to the building's exterior to make it pleasing to the eye; to make it noticeable and memorable. It's also part of the interior design."

"So the green band is exterior glass like the rest of the façade?"

"Yes. It projects from the plane of the front by one foot to create a pleasing shadow line."

I didn't know what a shadow line was but I didn't interrupt.

Andi nodded then cocked her head to the side. If we weren't all going to be monster chow, I would have considered it cute. Her head snapped up. "It's on the same electrical system as the rest of the building?"

"Of course," Krone said.

"They why did I see a green glow?"

Krone shrugged. "Emergency lights."

"Forgive me, Mr. Krone, but there are emergency lights on this floor and every floor. I don't think they would make the fog glow the same way the…what did you call it? Gingerbread? Horizontal element?"

"Maybe you just imagined it," Krone said.

"She didn't," the professor said. "I've known her for a long time. If she said she saw it, then she saw it."

"I have another question," Andi said. "That green band is at the thirteenth floor?"

"Yes, but—"

"I'm not being superstitious, Mr. Krone. On our way up the elevator, I noticed that there was no button for the thirteenth floor. Is that to make visitors more comfortable?"

"No. Not at all. I know there have been those who label the thirteenth floor as fourteen, but we've never done that. People aren't that superstitious anymore."

"Then why is there no access from the elevator?"

"The space isn't rentable. Much of the building's heating, cooling, electrical, and similar systems are on that floor. Of course, some of it has to be roof mounted, but we've found a way to make utilities more efficient if placed in the lower third of the building. Well, Jonathan Waterridge made all that work. I specialize in design; he specializes in mechanical matters in buildings. The man is brilliant in that area. Far more than I. Just like Ebony Watt excels in interior design."

Andi pressed on. "The name of the building is Portal Bay Front Plaza. Why that name?"

"Marketing, mostly." Krone said. "Buildings need to sound attractive as well as look beautiful. We're close to the the bay, so Bay Front. The bay is a port, so portal."

That made sense to me. It didn't make sense to Andi. "If that's the case, Mr. Krone, then shouldn't the name be Port Bay Front Plaza—not Portal."

Krone stared at her a minute. So did I. I wasn't following her logic. Lucky for me, Andi jumped right into an explanation:

"A port is a city where ships dock. A portal is a large gateway."

"And gateways lead from one place to another." The professor looked ill.

We thought on Andi's comment for a moment, then Brenda asked, "Has anyone seen Waterridge lately?"

DESPERATE TIMES REQUIRE DESPERATE ACTS

BRENDA'S QUESTION WAS a good one. I hadn't seen Waterridge since much earlier that evening. Turns out no one had. Of course, we had had other things to think about. Janice Krone slipped away and asked some of the firm's employees and Ebony Watt if they had seen the third partner. Nothing doing there either. A sick thought came to me. "Do you suppose he was one of those who went down one of the stairwells?"

Apparently I wasn't the first to think that. Allen Krone was the most doubtful. "He never seemed the kind of man to panic. If anything, he would try to keep people from panicking."

"I don't like to be disagreeable," the professor said. Brenda, Andi, and I almost gave ourselves whiplash looking at him. He frowned at us. "I'm a pretty good judge of character and something seemed off about the man."

Brenda started to address the "pretty good judge of character" comment but I shook my head. No doubt she was thinking of the same instances when the professor's keen mind missed the boat on character assessment. For once she took a hint from me. Probably because her fortunetelling wall art said I was going to be grub for those fog-swimmers.

"What makes you say that?" Andi asked.

"It's a gut feeling."

"Well, that's logical." One can keep Brenda quiet for only so long.

He didn't snap back which ended the theologian's debate about miracles happening in the contemporary world.

"The brain is always picking up information and details. If we know how to use our brain…" here he paused to make eye contact with Brenda, "…we can find clues we first missed."

I positioned myself to block Brenda should she decide to go for the professor's throat.

"I saw him."

The voice made me blink. It was Daniel and he was looking up at the tall adults (we often think of him as the little adult).

"When?" I asked.

He shrugged. Daniel wasn't good with time. "You were on the roof."

"So that's where you went, you sneaky little rascal."

"Did I do a bad thing?" He asked Brenda.

The first part of Brenda's answer was the sadness on her face; the second part was a grin; the third part had words. "Nah, actually, I'm kinda proud."

"What was he doing, buddy?" My gut told me this was important. The professor listened to his brain, I tend to eavesdrop on my gut.

"Standing over there." Daniel pointed across the room to the western most corner. "He was looking at the fog. He was looking at them."

Daniel was opening up. He did that sometimes. Usually when we need his help. Otherwise it was one word answers and video games.

"They were looking at him?" I had seen that look and it scared the wits out of me. "How do you know the fog-things were looking at Mr. Waterridge?"

"I walked over there. I already said I saw him."

"Yes, you did pal. My bad." I waited a half second before firing another. "You went over to him?"

Daniel nodded. "I looked at what he was looking at. The monsters were swimming in a circle looking at him."

"Looking at him." It wasn't a question. It was me echoing what Daniel said.

"I think they like him." Daniel inched closer to Brenda.

"Yeah, just like I like baloney sandwiches," Krone said.

"No. Not like—that. Like a dog."

Brenda, who spoke better Daniel than any of us took that one. "Like a dog? You mean like a dog looks at his owner."

"Uh-huh."

"My brain hurts." I looked at Andi. "Do your thing, girl. Pull it all together. Patternize what we know."

"Patternize?" The professor said. "Is that a word?"

"Don't mess with me, Professor. "I'll choose a better word later." Back to Andi. "You know what I mean. What is the pattern? How does all this connect? I need to hear it."

Andi closed her eyes. "Okay. New building. Midrise. Fifty floors but two are below grade. FAA limits height. Major earthquake. Weird fog rolls in. Aftershocks. Monsters swimming in the fog. Impossible—scratch that. It doesn't matter if it's impossible, it's being done." She sucked in a lung full of air. "Fog is rising. Fog is inside the building. It will be here soon. No thirteenth floor—no floor labeled thirteen. No common access to the floor. Mechanical space. Waterridge responsible for that part of the design. Building's name: Portal Bay Front Plaza. Portal not Port. Portal means gateway—Gate. The Gate."

The professor groaned. We had fought the Gate at every turn and come close to death every time. We know so little about them, but they have a plan for this world and it ain't good. To make things worse, there are people in this world helping them, maybe even guiding them. We believe some of them are part of a parallel universe, one that is close to ours but different. The professor says some physicists believe such places exist.

If I could have mustered the strength, I would have joined him.

"I don't follow," Krone said.

"It's a long story and a little too weird to believe," the professor said.

"I'm a dying man in a building I designed, surrounded by an impossible fog with killer creatures in it. Do you think you can tell me something I can't believe?"

"You might be surprised." The professor looked at us. We nodded.

I added a comment. "I've heard this story before. I need to think."

I wandered the floor trying to sort out what was rattling in my head. Something had to be done but what. We couldn't go down the stairs or the elevator. That was certain death and we had plenty of proof of that.

I did a few more slow laps around the big room and came to a conclusion. I had an idea. An idea I hated.

The walk back to my friends seemed like a hike through five feet of snow. I was chilled to the marrow. I had been walking around the perimeter of the room doing my best not to look out the window. My best wasn't good enough. I checked the rising fog repeatedly and it was climbing the building faster than I thought possible. It was just two or three floors below us. Pure. White. Soft. Deadly fog. Fog populated by big-headed, big-mouthed creatures with sharp teeth and claws, and a very real appetite for people.

I returned to my friends. No one had left. Allen Krone looked more stunned than before but that was understandable, if the professor had let him in on our little secret about the group we called the Gate. They had tried to do us in before. Worse, they had been trying to do in the world.

"Feel better after your little walk?" Brenda asked.

"No." It took a second or two to work up the courage to make my next statement. "I have an idea. I don't like it, and you're not going to like it either."

The moment I finished the sentence I felt something new. It came through the floor, into my feet, and up my legs. This time it wasn't an earthquake.

"What's that?" Andi looked on the verge of panic—and Andi doesn't panic.

The vibration increased and with it a noise that could be felt more than heard. There was no way we could stand this much longer. I'm no architect, but judging by the look on Krone's face, the building might not make it.

I put my big hands on Andi's little shoulders and looked deep in her eyes. I had to raise my voice. "Andi, you left one thing out of your summary. You forgot something."

She shook her head. "I didn't forget, Tank. None of us did. I just couldn't say it."

I hugged her for a long moment. It was the only thing that had felt right all day. Letting her go was the hardest thing I had done in a long time. Perhaps more difficult than what I was about to do.

"I'm going to do this," I said. "I don't want to hear objections, or anyone saying, 'But Tank.' We just don't have time." I turned my attention to Krone. "Mr. Krone, you know the mayor, right?"

"Yes."

"Are you friends?"

"Yes. For years."

Good. "So he trusts you."

"I believe so."

Good again. "I need you to ask him for a favor…"

ONE GIANT STEP FOR HUMANKIND

I HAD BEEN right. No one liked the plan, and even though I told them I wouldn't listen to objections, they objected anyway. Fortunately, I'm big enough to keep anyone from standing in my way.

There were hugs all around and then they dispersed to do what I asked. In less than ten minutes we were on the roof, not just my friends, but everyone. No one wanted to stay in a room that was vibrating like the inside of a bass drum. Several of the men in the group pitched in. The mayor's body guards were smooth, efficient, and strong. They managed to open the roof top storage room I had seen on my last trip to the roof.

It didn't take long to set up the window cleaning equipment. Krone had explained it all before. The building was designed with what he called davit supports. The davit, it turns out, is something I'd call a crane. Smaller of course than a crane used to build a building, but big enough to hold a window washer's basket, the kind that hold two men.

We wouldn't be needing the basket thing.

I slipped into the safety harness the workers wore when they cleaned the windows. We had to let out the belts as much as possible and it was still a tight fit. I would just have to live with the pinching. Or, if we understood Brenda's drawing, die with the pinching.

The creatures below noticed us working near the edge of the building and had worked themselves into a frenzy. I kept hoping they'd turn on each other. No good. Apparently they like the flavor of human more.

"I've rechecked my calculations." Krone stood beside me looking at the davit and the safety line we attached to it. "The length should be right."

"Should be?" I needed a little more optimism.

"Sorry." It looked like he tried to smile but his lips misfired. He did manage to look scared out of his wits. I didn't want to know how I looked. "Speech patterns are difficult to break. Architects learn to speak with caution. Did you know that malpractice insurance for architects is more expensive than that for doctors?"

"Are you stalling, Mr. Krone?"

"Yes, yes I am." This time his smile worked just fine.

One of the mayor's bodyguards moved closer. "Are you sure about this?"

"Not at all," I said. "I'm doing it anyway."

"I spent ten years in the marine corps and have seen many acts of bravery," the bodyguard said. "This one takes the cake."

"I don't feel brave." It was an honest admission.

"Bravery is defined by what you do, not what you feel." He shook my hand then pulled a handgun from beneath his tux coat. "The mayor said you wanted one of these."

"Thanks."

"You know how to use it?"

"It's a Glock 9 mm." I pulled the slide, putting a round in the chamber. "I have an uncle who is a sheriff. Any visit to his place would sooner or later end up on the shooting range." I didn't tell him, I'm not big on guns.

"You know there are more of those creatures than there are bullets in that piece."

"The gun isn't for them." I let that hang in the air. There was too much talk and I was losing my nerve.

The professor laid a hand on my shoulder. In his other hand he held a fire axe. The kind with a blade on one side and a point on the other. It was in a cabinet near each of the stairwells.

"Tank—" The professor choked, cleared his throat then tried again. "Tank, I've been rough on you, but I want you to know—"

"Stop, Professor. I don't want the girls to see me get all emotional and stuff." I took the axe.

He patted my shoulder and walked away.

I was done talking. Every minute that passed brought the fog closer. Every minute that passed took a little of my spine with it.

No more waiting. I closed my eyes and took several deep breaths. I tightened the muscles in my left arm, then my right; I did the same for each leg. More deep breathing. It was the way I got ready for a football game. It was the only thing I knew to do.

I stepped on the parapet, careful of my balance. I needed to leave the roof in a particular way. Falling wasn't the way.

I glanced back at my friends and saw tears in their eyes. I looked down at the pale demons in the fog, then I turned my eyes to heaven. "Father, this is stupid but it is the only thing I know to do. Help me do it."

I crouched, then leaned forward. With all the strength I could muster I sprang into the nothing screaming all the way. The moment I exchanged the solid roof for the air I twisted so my back was to the fog.

The sky overhead disappeared in a blanket of white. That didn't matter, I was looking for green.

Something zipped by but missed—almost missed. It had scratched my arm. In the few seconds of free fall I had, I saw dozens of the creatures. They swooped at me, but missed me each time. They would have had better luck catching a falling meteor.

Green.

I raised my gun. My trajectory had changed. I was no longer falling. Instead, I was swinging right into the building. I extended the Glock in my left hand and fired, and fired, and fired. The sound was much louder than any gun I had ever heard. The creatures diving at me disappeared as if the noise hurt them. Fine with me.

I continued to fire. I had been told the weapon had ten rounds. I tested that by firing until the gun went silent. I released it.

Allen Krone told me the glass skin was made of a type of tempered glass. Very durable. Very strong.

But not bullet proof. The glass would shatter into small cubes. He was correct.

My momentum swung me through the spot where one of the green windows had been. The next part was going to be tricky. Somehow I had to stop my swing once I sailed through the window area. That's what the axe was for.

The lights on the floor were in full force. All green, but in full force. Outside, the fog, which was now inside, was white. Here it was a moss green gas.

When I felt my direction change my shoes were one or two feet above the floor. I rocked forward and drove the pointed end of the axe into the floor. Krone told me the floors in the building were made of something called light-weight concrete. Concrete with air blown in it to make it less dense and heavy. It was a good thing it wasn't ordinary concrete. I doubt my axe would have made much of an impression. As it was I could only drive the end of the axe about an inch into the surface. It was enough. I had stopped my wild swing. I let go of the handle and a swung back a couple more feet, just enough for my feet to set down.

No sooner than I had touched down I began to unclip the safety line. I had to try three times before I could unleash myself. The harness swung back through the shattered window, and into a swarm of fog-swimmers. They attacked it.

I yanked the fire axe free and turned to face the things that wanted me for tonight's dinner. I steeled myself for the onslaught. I had the advantage of speed when I leapt from the building and the sudden change of direction when I reached the end of my safety line. That was then. Now, I was standing flatfooted in dress shoes and a tux, hardly fighting clothes. The floor, the walls, the machinery all buzzed and vibrated, just like the vibration we felt right before I committed to this mission.

The charging swirling swarm of creatures didn't come. They stayed outside the building, swimming past the area of the shattered window. They didn't come in. They just stared at me like I was the ugly one, a fish in a tank.

I would like to have sat and pondered what kept them outside but I didn't think I had the time. They might change their minds—if they have minds.

That's when it occurred to me, I was breathing the fog and it felt like any other fog I'd been in. I'm not sure what I expected, I was just glad to be breathing. I backed away from the window and tried to make sense of my surroundings. This was supposed to be an equipment floor and sure enough, there was equipment. There were large metal structures that were a mystery to me. Big cylindrical tanks like giant propane tanks. They were a mystery to me to. Overhead were conduits, pipes, ducts and, yep, more things that were a mystery to me.

What I was looking for had to be different. I didn't know how. A sudden fear, a new fear gripped me, what if I couldn't find the whatever it was I was looking for? What if it was disguised to look like a refrigerator or somethin' else familiar.

No, it had to be obvious. If we were right, if Andi and I linked everything together, then the Gate had set up a portal on this floor—a portal to their world. I don't think you can hide something like that.

I moved slowly around the floor not certain what I was looking for, but certain I'd recognize it. Every few steps I looked behind me, fully expecting to see one of the blood splattered faces of those critters. Brenda's drawing played in my mind. Not somethin' I enjoyed.

I studied the ceiling again and this time I noticed that the green light was not uniform. It was brighter to my left and further back. I made that my destination.

My steps were slow and I peeked around every machine fearing what I might see, then I saw a movement near the western most wall.

A figure.

A man.

A man in a red robe.

There was something familiar about the robe. I had seen something similar before.

The figure stood at a console of some kind. To his right was an opening the size of a garage door. The opening was sealed with green glass. As I drew closer, I could see one fog-swimmer after another falling through a green mist. I corrected myself. Not falling. Swimming down to someplace lower. Maybe the underground parking floors.

The vibration increased. The noise was deafening, which is probably why the man in the robe hadn't heard the window shatter.

He spun suddenly. Looked at me, and reached for something inside the robe. It was Waterridge, and he had a gun.

He raised it.

I threw the axe in his direction. I wasn't trying to hit him. I was trying to hit the control panel, and maybe buy enough time for me to move closer.

He dove to the side and covered his head. There was the time I needed. The axe hit the control panel and bounced off. No damage to the panel. No damage to the axe.

Waterridge had dropped his weapon. Apparently seeing a firefighter's axe flying at his head had broken his concentration. It had skittered several feet beyond his reach. He began a desperate crawl for it. I got there before he did, grabbed the gun and stuck it in my pocket. I needed both hands for what I had to do next.

I retrieved the axe and studied the panel for a moment. Metal conduit, hollow aluminum pipes, ran from the panel up the wall and into the ceiling. I laid into them with the axe.

"No!" Waterridge struggled to his feet.

Sparks flew. The vibration stopped. And the portal with its streams of creepy things and fog went empty. A few creatures who had been swimming down the fog filled channel, now dropped like stones.

The vibration stopped too. I was glad for that. For a moment.

"You've killed us." Waterridge struggled to his feet.

"Sorry, pal, but the way I see it, I kept you from killing thousands of other people."

"You're a fool!"

"Sticks and stones." That's when I noticed it. There was a screech. Just one at first. Then another. Then several.

"How did you get in here?" Waterridge stepped closer and I wondered if I was going to have to deck the guy.

"Through the window. It was recommended that I not take the stairs. I think you know why."

"We're doomed."

Another screech.

Waterridge was just a decibel two or so shy of screaming. "They'll get in. The sound, the vibration is what kept them from this floor."

Uh-oh. "Why aren't they here?"

"They're not smart. They don't reason. They don't discuss things and make conjectures, you idiot. They are purely reactive. They're sharks in bloody water. No reasoning. They're flying piranha in a frenzy. It will only take seconds for them to realize they can come in now."

He was right.

Boy, was he right.

At first there was just one. I spied his bulbous white head peeking around a large piece of machinery. It moved slowly. A lion stalking. A killer whale eyeing seals. A shark circling. They might not be reasoning creatures but they seemed to understand self preservation.

I pushed Waterridge to the side and retrieved his gun from my pocket. A .22 caliber. I would have preferred something a little heftier. I pointed at the scout. He wasn't alone. Another head appeared.

"Shoot!"

"Not yet." There was no way this little gun held enough ammo to take on the hundreds of creatures that lurked in the fog. I could take down a few. Maybe a half-dozen if my aim was good. Maybe. Doubtful. It didn't matter. Brenda's prophetic drawing had already told me my fate.

"Shoot!"

"Aren't you supposed to have some control over these things? You got the red robe and everything."

"You put an end to that when you cut the power to my control panel. You doomed us."

"You doomed thousands."

The first creature floated through the fog. Several more appeared behind them and they were showing signs of being less patient.

I pulled the trigger and the bullet slammed into the head of the first one around the corner. I expected blood. Instead I saw a spray of yellow custard. If fear hadn't occupied most of my brain, I would have tossed chunks right then and there.

The others scattered, more from the sound of the gun than the death of their companion.

Motion from the portal window caught my attention. Last I looked creatures were falling past, now they were rising, sucked up to wherever the wide shaft went.

The first one's up were the last one's down. They were battered and broken. Dead. Then I saw a living one struggling against the flow. He was trying to swim down the fog column but the riptide was too strong.

An idea started to grow but Waterridge stunted its growth. He charged me and seized my gun hand.

"Let me have it." I saw nothing but panic in his eyes.

I dropped the axe in my other hand and popped the architect in the nose. He staggered back two steps.

Something on the ceiling moved. I looked up. They clung to the ceiling tiles, claws holding them in place. There—were—hundreds of them, a quivering mass of putty-white bodies, their heads turned our direction, each mouth filled with barracuda teeth.

Waterridge took another step back. "No. No." He raised his hands. "I command you to leave."

That didn't work. One dropped on his head and dug its claws into his eyes. The scream, echoed in the room. I considered shooting the thing on his head but I could miss and blow the man's brains out. For a moment—God forgive me—for a moment it seemed the right thing to do.

Then one hit me in the back. They were coming at us from every direction. I drove myself back against the wall. Something squished. My back felt wet.

Another came at me flying five feet above the floor. I dropped it with a shot from the .22. Fighting was useless but I wasn't wired to stand around.

Waterridge was on the ground, writhing. Then the screaming stopped. Then the writhing stopped. All that was left was the sound of the feeding frenzy.

A creature hit me in the side. His claws ripped through my dress shirt. My skin offered no resistance. One bit my arm. Another laid into my leg. I went down on my back. For every creature that dropped from the ceiling another appeared to replace it. There were five on me. Then more.

I fought. I punched. I shot one or two more. My blood flowed and with it my ability to fend off the beasts.

Again, a motion in the portal demanded my attention. Creatures were being sucked up the shaft by the dozen...

I still held the gun. I could still see out of one eye. It took everything I had to move my arm enough to aim. The sound of the gun sent the creatures on me scrambling, but they would be back in a moment.

I fired again. And again. Then I could hear only the sound of dry firing. I was out of ammo. The glass had cracked but not broken.

I rolled on my side. There was the fire axe two steps out of reach. Crawling to it, I took in in my right hand. My left wasn't working very well.

A creature landed on my back. I was beyond caring. "I hope you choke."

Using the axe for support I pushed myself up. Another foggy latched on. I stumbled but at least I stumbled in the right direction. Several more creatures hitched a ride. One thing I had noticed about them; they were very light. I guess you'd have to be to swim in fog.

This was it. My last effort. The last thing I would do in this life. I refused to waste it. The biting and clawing increased. The frenzy was beginning.

I lifted the axe, turned the pointed end out and put my body into the swing.

The axe head bounced off the glass and the axe fell to the floor.

"I tried, God. I tried."

The glass gave way, its pieces imploding into the shaft. Wind. I felt wind. Then I keeled over.

There were screeches. The air whistled through the room and around the edges of the portal. One by one, then two by two, then by bunches, the creatures were pulled into the open portal. I couldn't tell if it was the wind or something else dragging them away. I didn't care as long as they left. They made it clear they didn't want to go.

The fog that filled the room went with them. It was like watching milky water go down a drain, or up a drain.

The fog-swimmers clinging to me sloughed off. Glad to see them go. I turned to where Waterridge had gone down. There were still bits and pieces of him left.

For a few moments I watched fog and creatures sail by, but keeping my eyes open was becoming more work than I could manage.

"I'm ready, God. I'm ready...to...go..."

The green and the white of the room dimmed to black.

Epilogue

"HOW ARE YOU doing, son?" Allen Krone walked onto the balcony and sat in one of the outdoor chairs. He had a right to. He owned the chair, the balcony, and the eight thousand square foot house over looking the Pacific Ocean. The house was in the northern part of San Diego county. We had been here for two weeks and had full run of the place. Krone and his wife stayed in one of their other homes.

"I'm doing okay, sir."

"It looks like you're healing up nicely." Janice brought a tray of ice tea for her husband, me, and my friends. Krone did a lot of entertaining he had said, so there were plenty of chairs. Daniel sat on the deck playing a video game on his phone.

"It's slow, but I shouldn't frighten too many children."

I wore shorts and a white t-shirt. The scars on my neck, arms, and legs were visible reminders of what had happened earlier that month. The rest of the scars were hidden by clothing. I'd be wearing long sleeve shirts and long pants for a good many months. The plastic surgeons told me the scars will fade, and those that don't can be handled with a little surgery. Somehow that didn't seem important.

I studied our host for a moment. "You're looking pretty good yourself, Mr. Krone."

"I keep telling you its, Allen. And I feel good. Thanks to you."

"Not me, sir. God does the healing. I'm just a washed up football jock."

"Not in my book, young man." Krone looked over the ocean as if seeing something no one else could. "You are the bravest man I know. Your friends too."

"Eh, they're all right, I guess." That got a reaction.

"I thought we had lost you," Andi said. She kept her eyes closed and her face toward the sun.

"I thought I had lost me, too."

I don't remember my friends finding me, but they tell me they came looking when the fog disappeared. To be honest, I still have trouble understanding how I can be alive.

It had taken some time before we could discuss what had happened. I was in a hospital in the north county of San Diego when I came to. Two of the guests at the retirement party were RNs. They stopped the bleeding. Once the fog was completely gone and we were able to contact others, Krone had his private helicopter jet in from Montgomery Field enough miles out of downtown San Diego not to be affected by the fog.

"Any word from the mayor on the city's condition," I asked. I didn't want to talk about me anymore. I find myself boring.

"He's being tightlipped about such things. They can't explain the loss of life, the power outages. The official word is that this is an ongoing investigation. Local police, the military, the FBI, Homeland Security, and probably groups I know nothing about are investigating. There is no reasonable, logical answer."

"Trust me," the professor said. "I know reason. I know logic. Nothing of what we've experienced makes sense. It is, nonetheless, real."

"What do these people want?"

The professor always fielded those kinds of questions. "We're not certain. We've seen them try to control the thinking of people. At times it seems as if they want to make our universe theirs. This time they unleashed organisms to kill and to cause terror. They've also used microscopic organisms to infect people and animals." The professor shrugged. "I'm starting to wonder if our worlds aren't so different that we can't understand what they're doing. I know one thing: The Gate isn't finished with us."

"What I don't understand," Krone said, "is Brenda's gift. You told me she is never wrong, yet Tank didn't die."

"I've been thinking about that," Brenda said. "I've been pretty bummed about gettin' that wrong."

"Hey!" I smiled when I said it.

"You know what I mean, Cowboy. I've grown...oh, what's the word?"

"Fond of me," I suggested.

"No, that's not it. Gimme a sec. Got it. I've grown to were I can *tolerate* you. That's it. Anyway, I think I have an answer. I'll let the professor tell you if I'm right or wrong. He's going to anyway."

"You can count on it, Barnick."

"I think Tank changed the future. What I drew was true. Tank made a new truth. I don't know how. Maybe he just powered his way into a different outcome."

"That's deep," the professor said. "Especially coming from you. Just like some physicist think there are multiple universes, there may be multiple futures."

Changed the future. As I thought about Brenda's words, it occurred to me that that's what we've been doing all along. Changing the future.

I caught the professor looking at me. "I'm glad Tank is still with us."

"Aw, gee, Professor. You're gonna make me blush."

"Don't get a big head, Tank. I just don't want to be left alone with these two women."

"You love us too," Andi said.

Brenda was a little more direct. "Shut up, old man."

"For the last time, I am not old!"

"Ancient."

I'll let you guess who said that.

BOOKS BY ALTON GANSKY

FICTION

By My Hands

Through My Eyes

Terminal

Tarnished Image

Marked for Mercy

A Small Dose of Murder

A Ship Possessed

Vanished

Distant Memory

The Prodigy

Dark Moon

A Treasure Deep

Out of Time

Beneath the Ice

The Incumbent

Before Another Dies

Submerged

Director's Cut

Crime Scene Jerusalem

Zero-G

Finder's Fee

Angel

Enoch

Wounds

The Girl

The Fog

COLLABORATIVE FICTION

The Bell Messenger, with Bob Cornuke

Certain Jeopardy, with Jeff Struecker

The Pravda Messenger, with Bob Cornuke

Blaze of Glory, with Major Jeff Struecker

Mayan Apocalypse, with Dr. Mark Hitchcock

Fallen Angel, with Major Jeff Struecker

Scroll, with Grant Jeffery

Hide and Seek, with Jeff Struecker

Digital Winter, with Dr. Mark Hitchcock

NONFICTION

Uncovering the Bible's Greatest Mysteries

Uncovering God's Mysterious Ways

40 Days

In His Words

What Really Matters Most

The Indispensable Guide to Jesus

Conversations with God

60 People Who Shaped the Church

30 Events that Shaped the Church

NONFICTION CO-AUTHOR

The Secrets God Kept, with John Van Deist

The Solomon Secret, with Bruce Fleet

FROM HARBINGERS 9
THE LEVIATHAN

BILL MYERS

ABOUT ALTON L. GANSKY

Alton L. Gansky (Al) is the author of 24 novels and nine nonfiction works, as well as principal writer of nine novels and two nonfiction books. He has been a Christy Award finalist (*A Ship Possessed*) and an Angel Award winner (*Terminal Justice*) and recently received the ACFW award for best suspense/thriller for his work on *Fallen Angel*. He holds a BA and MA in biblical studies and was granted a Litt.D. He lives in central California with his wife.

www.altongansky.com

Catch up on all the Harbingers episodes!

CPSIA information can be obtained at www.ICGtesting.com
Printed in the USA
LVOW10s2158240816

501735LV00014B/283/P